What is the dark-thirty?

"When I was growing up in the South, we kids called the half hour just before nightfall the dark-thirty. We had exactly half an hour to get home before the monsters came out," writes Patricia C. McKissack in her introduction to this collection of ghostly tales. All of the stories in it are pure McKissack—inspired by the oral storytelling tradition that was part of her childhood, yet totally original. She recommends that these stories be shared "at that special time when it is neither day nor night and when shapes and shadows play tricks on the mind. When you feel fear tingling in your toes and zinging up your spine like a closing zipper, you have experienced the delicious horror of a tale of the dark-thirty."

Patricia C. McKissack has written many other award-winning children's books, such as *Mirandy and Brother Wind, Nettie Jo's Friends,* and *A Million Fish . . . More or Less,* and has collaborated with her husband, Fredrick, on such notable works of nonfiction as their Coretta Scott King Award winner *A Long Hard Journey: The Story of the Pullman Porter*. They live in St. Louis and have two grown sons.

Brian Pinkney's hauntingly beautiful illustrations for *The Dark-Thirty* are the perfect complement to Ms. McKissack's text. Mr. Pinkney's unusual scratchboard drawings can also be seen in *The Ballad of Belle Dorcas* by William H. Hooks, the 1994 illustrated edition of Langston Hughes's classic *The Dream Keeper,* and the 1996 Caldecott Honor Book *The Faithful Friend* by Robert D. San Souci. He lives with his wife, Andrea Davis Pinkney, a children's book author with whom he often collaborates, in Brooklyn.

Patricia C. McKissack

Illustrated by
Brian Pinkney

ALFRED A. KNOPF NEW YORK

To my grandmother, Sarah Jane James

—P. C. M.

To my wife, Andrea

—B. P.

THIS IS A BORZOI BOOK PUBLISHED BY ALFRED A. KNOPF, INC.

Published in the United States by Alfred A. Knopf, Inc., New York, and simultaneously in Canada by Random House of Canada Limited, Toronto. Distributed by Random House, Inc., New York.

Originally published in hardcover as a Borzoi Book by Alfred A. Knopf, Inc., in 1992.

Book design by Mina Greenstein

http://www.randomhouse.com/

Library of Congress Cataloging-in-Publication Data
McKissack, Pat.
The dark-thirty : southern tales of the supernatural / by Patricia C. McKissack ; illustrated by Brian Pinkney. p. cm.
Summary: A collection of ghost stories with African American themes, designed to be told during the dark-thirty—the half hour before sunset—when ghosts seem all too believable.
ISBN 0-679-81863-4 (trade)
ISBN 0-679-91863-9 (lib. bdg.)
ISBN 0-679-88335-5 (pbk.)
1. Ghost stories, American. 2. Horror tales, American. 3. Afro-Americans—Juvenile fiction. 4. Children's stories, American. [1. Ghost—Fiction. 2. Horror stories. 3. Afro-Americans—Fiction. 4. Short stories.] I. Pinkney, J. Brian, ill. II. Title.
PZ7.M478693Tah 1992 [Fic]—dc20 92-3021

Printed in the United States of America 10 9 8 7 6 5 4 3 2 1

About the illustrations
The artwork in this book was done in scratchboard, a technique in which a white board is covered with black ink. The ink is then scratched off with a sharp tool to reveal the white underneath. Color for the jacket was added with oil pastels, which were rubbed into the scratched lines.

Author's Note

WHEN I WAS GROWING UP in the South, we kids called the half hour just before nightfall the dark-thirty. We had exactly half an hour to get home before the monsters came out.

During the hot, muggy summer, when days last longer, we gathered on the front porch to pass away the evening hours. Grandmama's hands were always busy, but while shelling peas or picking greens, she told a spine-chilling ghost tale about Laughing Lizzy, a specter who'd gone mad after losing her entire family in a fire. Her hysterical laughter was said to drive listeners insane.

Then on cold winter nights, when the dark-thirty came early, our family sat in the living room and talked. The talk generally led to one of Grandmama's hair-raising tales. As the last glimmers of light faded from the window overlooking the woods, she told about Gray Jim, the runaway slave who'd been killed while trying to escape. Gray Jim's ghost haunted the woods on moonless nights. "Sorry for those who hear Gray Jim's dying screams," she whispered, " 'cause they're not long for this world." At this point my grandmother would pause and say, "Pat, go in the kitchen and get me a glass of water."

Many years later I learned that Laughing Lizzy and Gray Jim had been real people in our small African American community. The strange—and often sad—circumstances of their deaths had inspired the ghost stories that lived after them. They inspired me, too.

The Dark-Thirty: Southern Tales of the Supernatural is a collection of original stories rooted in African American history and the oral storytelling tradition. They should be shared at that special time when it is neither day nor night and when shapes and shadows play tricks on the mind. When you feel fear tingling in your toes and zinging up your spine like a closing zipper, you have experienced the delicious horror of a tale of the dark-thirty.

Patricia C. McKissack
1992

Contents

The Legend of Pin Oak

In 1868 a Kentucky artist, Thomas Satterwhite Noble, painted *The Price of Blood,* which shows the sale of a mulatto slave by his father-master, to illustrate the cruelty of slavery. There is no greater horror than a system that allows parents to sell their children—or, as in this story, brother to sell brother.

THE PLANTATION BELL summoned everybody to the big house. About fifty slaves, including the inside help, gathered in front of the white mansion. Among them were Henri and his wife, Charlemae.

Harper McAvoy, looking pale and weak, stood beside one of the big Doric columns that supported the second-story porch. After nervously clearing his throat, he announced in a not-so-steady voice, "I've sold Henri."

One of the slaves screamed, Charlemae perhaps, Harper didn't know for sure. As he hurried back inside the house voices called after him:

"No, not Henri."

"Massa! What about Charlemae and the baby?"

"Who will see after things round here?"

"What will become of us all . . . ?"

Harper raced to his study, where he barricaded himself against the onslaught of questions. "I sold Henri!" he said, giggling foolishly. "I did it! Now I'll be rid of him."

Suddenly the door to his study burst open. "Do you hate me that much?" Henri asked without hesitation. "Enough to destroy Pin Oak?"

Harper scurried behind his desk to put a barrier between them. "I owe you no explanation. You're my slave!"

HARPER'S resentment of Henri began in childhood. Actually their story started with Amos McAvoy, the former master of Pin Oak. Amos had inherited the estate from his father, Thomas McAvoy, who had built it the same year Thomas Jefferson was elected President of the United States. Only Andrew Jackson's Hermitage equaled Pin Oak's graceful architectural styling and elegant setting.

Amos McAvoy had been a tall, red-headed man with a square-cut chin and deep-set green eyes. He'd courted the lovely Alva Dean from Spring Manor and won her over with his dashing style and devil-may-care charm. Their spring wedding united two old Tennessee families—the Deans and the McAvoys—two fortunes and two hearts. But the marriage lasted only a year.

The night they told Amos that Alva had died in childbirth, he locked himself in her room and wept bitterly. When Amos finally emerged the next morning, he named his son Harper, then abandoned Pin Oak, leaving it to be run by overseers.

For ten years Harper saw Amos only a few weeks during harvest season. The rest of the time his father stayed in New Orleans. The boy was left in the charge of his grandmother Dean, who showered him with everything her money could buy. But material possessions and her love were no substitute for the thing he most desired—his father's acceptance.

"He would rather I had died," Harper told his grandmother. And no matter how much Amanda Dean tried to deny it, they both knew it was true. To ease his pain, Harper taught himself not to care.

Then one day Amos unexpectedly arrived at the Deans' Spring Manor. Harper slipped down the steps and stood outside the parlor, where he listened to the conversation.

"I'm returning to Pin Oak," Amos said. "And I want my son to come live with me."

"There's nothing I can do to stop you," Amanda answered coldly. "But why now after all these years? You've never taken the slightest interest in the boy before."

"I know. And it was wrong," he admitted, "but I plan to make it up. I've left my affairs in the care of others far too long."

Amanda sighed deeply. "Harper is a complicated child—I don't think he knows how to be happy. I've spoiled him, I know. Perhaps it will be good for him to be with you."

"Yes, from now on things will be better."

HARPER had lived at Pin Oak for about a month when his father announced that he was going to New Orleans. He returned several weeks later with Henri, a mulatto child about two years younger than Harper.

The boy had a mop of dark red hair, a square chin, and unusual pale green eyes. Gossip spread quickly from the big house to the quarters.

"Say the boy's mama was one of them free blacks down in New Orleans," Harper overheard the cook tell the driver.

"Got his mama's skin and his daddy's green eyes—an odd combination."

"That's for sure. Anybody with eyes can clearly see that Henri is Massa Amos's own flesh and blood."

Harper saw what everybody else saw. The McAvoys were big, strong, athletic men with ruddy complexions. Henri, though younger, was taller and more solidly built than Harper. A frail child with the same pastel features as his mother, Harper hated the way he looked and despised Henri for looking so much like *their father.*

What was worse, Amos never denied a word of the gossip. Even if he had, it wouldn't have stopped the tongues from wagging.

"So it's all true," Amanda Dean gasped when she came to Pin Oak, admittedly to see Henri. She fell into a chair and fanned herself, then turned to Amos. "You and that boy are the talk of two counties. Now I see why!"

Amos sent Henri on an errand so that he could speak freely to Amanda. "The child's mother is dead, and I didn't want him with somebody who might mistreat him."

"How dare you shame my grandson with this . . . this abomination? I've come to take Harper back to Spring Manor."

"No, the boy stays here," he answered. "Henri will be a good companion for Harper. I brought him home for that purpose."

"Are you so blind?" Amanda said, pointing an accusing finger. "This can only lead to disaster."

Amos ignored his mother-in-law's counsel and installed Henri as a house servant.

In time, however, Henri was put in charge of Amos's stables. Pin Oak's horses were some of the finest in the state, and Amos was a gifted horseman. Henri enjoyed taking care of Hercules, Amos's prize stallion. Harper, on the other hand, stayed as far from the stables as possible—horses made him sneeze, and riding them made him sore.

"I'm hot," Harper complained when Amos took both boys out to view the fields. "And besides, I'm not interested in how cotton grows."

"Stop whining, Harper," Amos scolded. "You'll be master of Pin Oak one day. And Henri, you'll run the place. That's the way I want it."

THE SEASONS passed swiftly, until at last Henri reached manhood, tall, confident, and strong. Harper's jealousy of Henri grew each year until it dominated his life, and he was immersed in an ever-widening pool of anger and hatred.

Just as Amos planned it, Henri was put in charge of Pin Oak operations. Soon after, Amos approved his marriage to Charlemae, a beautiful African woman. Together they built a cabin with a stone fireplace, wood floors, and shuttered windows. It wasn't until then that Amos told Henri he was free.

"Your mama was freed by her master when she was born. I never told you before now, because I didn't want you running off when you were too young to take care of yourself. You're twenty-five and the law says I have to let you go."

"I've always known I was free," Henri said. "My mama told me many times before she died."

"Will you be leaving Pin Oak?" Amos asked.

Henri sighed. "No, because Charlemae belongs to you, and she couldn't come with me. I'll stay and keep running Pin Oak—but for a salary. And I want to use that salary to buy Charlemae's freedom."

"A wise decision," Amos said, smiling.

As LONG AS Amos lived, Henri was safe. Then one Christmas, Amos took sick at the dinner table. Believing it to be indigestion brought on by too much eggnog, Henri helped Amos to his bedroom. By the time they realized it was something far worse, it was too late.

"He's asking for his son," Dr. Shipp said, turning first to Henri, then to Harper. After an embarrassing moment, the doctor said to Harper, "He's asking for you. Do hurry. He's near death."

Brushing past Henri, Harper went into his father's bedroom. "I'm here."

Amos held out his trembling hand, and for a split second Harper wanted to embrace his dying father and forget everything that had gone wrong between them. Instead he stood in stony silence. "Henri . . ." Amos struggled to say. "Tell him . . ." But Amos McAvoy died before he could finish.

"Henri to the last," Harper hissed. "Not even a parting word for me." He sat in the darkened room for a while. Then he started laughing, a chuckle that turned into a shrill giggle. When the doctor and Henri rushed in to see what was happening, Harper looked at them with wild eyes. "I am the master of Pin Oak."

"DID HE SAY anything about freeing Charlemae and my son?"

Henri asked some weeks after the funeral. "He promised Charlemae and me—"

"No. In fact, *my father* suggested I sell you," Harper lied. "But of course I'd keep Charlemae . . . and your baby. Does that bother you, Henri? Knowing you're just a slave after all?"

Harper looked for signs of hurt in Henri's face. He saw only his father's contemptuous green eyes staring defiantly back at him.

"Go, get out." Harper waved Henri away.

But his brother didn't leave. Though Henri saw no point in telling Harper he was a free man, there was another matter he needed to discuss. "There's something you should know," he said with urgency in his voice. "Pin Oak is in trouble."

"What kind of trouble?" Harper asked, growing nervous.

"For the past two years the crops haven't come in healthy—too much rain one year, not enough the next. Still, Master Amos said if we toed the line, cut a few corners, and brought in a good crop this year, we could get through these hard times."

Harper turned his back on Henri. "How dreary. Do what you must to keep the place going."

But meanwhile Harper continued to spend Pin Oak's money, on good whiskey and bad deals. It wasn't long before the bank threatened foreclosure.

Driven by years of anger and resentment, Harper met the bank's demand payment by selling the most valuable asset he had—Henri.

"You fool!" Mr. Kelsey, a longtime family friend at the bank, shouted when Harper told him. "Why didn't you sell the silver? Sell all the furniture? Not Henri. Would a carpenter sell his saw?"

BUT THE deed had been done. Harper sat in his office listening to a slave sing a mournful tune.

Steal away . . . steal away . . . steal away home.
I ain't got time to stay here . . .

He, too, longed to steal away to a peaceful place, if only for a moment. He drifted off to sleep.

"Harper."

Opening his eyes, Harper saw his father—no, it was only Henri. "Do you think you might try saying 'sir' or 'Massa Harper,' " he said sarcastically.

"I've come once more to plead with you to reconsider."

"Sorry, but there's nothing I can do. I sold you."

"But that's just it. You can't sell me," Henri said carefully. "I'm free, because my mother was free. You know the law. When my mother died, your father came to New Orleans to get me, but he knew the condition of my birth. That's why he couldn't sell me. Neither can you."

Harper's eyes stretched wide with anger and frustration. "Wh-where are your papers?" he asked incredulously. "Can you show me some papers?"

"Here."

Harper read the document and swore. "He never told me. You mean you were always free to go? Why didn't you just leave?"

"I couldn't abandon Charlemae and our baby. Besides, Master Amos was letting me build cash credits to buy my family's freedom. I should be close to my goal."

"I can't imagine my father making such a deal."

"Master Amos must have kept records. Won't you at least look?"

Harper ignored the question. He rubbed his temples. "The dealers are coming tomorrow," he whined. "Oh, they do terrible things to people who renege on sales. What must I do?"

"Give them their money back."

"I've spent it."

But slowly an idea formed in Harper's head. As it grew and took shape, he smiled. "Since you're free, I'll give them Charlemae in your place. If you want, you can follow her and offer your services to her new master. I'll keep your son, of course. That seems a fair deal, don't you think?"

"What? Why?"

"Why not? You always got everything you wanted. But now I'm in charge."

Henri started to walk away but turned back. "You always envied me, but there was no cause," he said. "How do you think I felt having to call my own father Massa Amos? I used to watch you whine and fret, and he'd remind you that one day you'd be master of Pin Oak. I ran Pin Oak for him, kept it afloat, but in the end he called you to his bedside." Henri shook his head. "You never understood." Then he left.

DAWN BROUGHT the slave dealers, as promised.

"Beautiful morning, don't you think?"

"We've come for the buck," one man said gruffly.

The other one took an ankle cuff and chain from his pack. "Fetch him."

"There's a slight problem . . ."

"We're listening."

"Unfortunately, Henri is a free man," Harper said apologetically. "Seems he was born free. The sale I made was illegal."

One of the men spat tobacco juice. "Whoever heard of a free nigger in Tennessee? We're taking him, papers or no. Go fetch him."

A nod from Harper sent a slave child scurrying toward the quarters. Within seconds he returned, yelling, "They gone. They gone!"

"Who's gone? Where?"

"Henri, Charlemae, and the boy. They gone. Cabin empty."

The dealers mounted quickly. "You got dogs?"

"I do."

"Get your horse. We'll track 'em." And they rode off.

"I don't ride," Harper called. "I'll be along in my carriage."

The men followed Henri and Charlemae through the orchards and along Topps River. Their trail was easy to follow. The dogs reached the clearing first. They had cornered their quarry.

The runaways had climbed a steep cliff and were huddled on a ledge jutting out over the crashing water. Their backs were to the falls, with no chance for escape.

The dogs barked and tried to climb the wet, slippery rocks. Henri called out to the lead dog. "Blue!" Hearing his voice, all the dogs stopped yelping and wagged their tails in friendly recognition.

The slave dealers bolted into the clearing. Harper followed minutes later.

"Come down from there, boy!"

"We got no time for this. There ain't no place else to run. So bring yourself down with the woman."

But instead of backing down, Henri and Charlemae inched forward to the edge of the cliff. Then, after handing the baby to Henri, Charlemae leaped into the water. A split second later, Henri, the boy clutched tightly to his chest, leaped too.

Harper scrambled from his carriage and struggled to climb the cliff. Finally reaching the spot where Henri had stood moments before, he looked down, and his frightened brown eyes searched the churning waters.

Suddenly, miraculously, Harper saw a large beautiful bird rise

out of the mists. It hovered overhead, circling. Another bird, a female, joined her mate. Screeching loudly, a fledgling flapped frantically to stay in flight. The parents waited patiently until the little one gained confidence. Once the three were airborne, the birds circled, then flew north.

"No," Harper cried. "Come back. Come back. You always win!" The ledge began to crumble. The men tried to call to him, warn him, but it was too late. The ground gave way, taking Harper McAvoy into the crashing waters below.

They found his body downstream. But they never found a trace of Henri, Charlemae, or their child. The authorities called Harper's death a terrible accident. The others were listed as suicides.

But the driver who had been part of the search told a different story. Down in the quarters, he told about a slave family who leaped into the Topps River Falls but weren't killed—they were transformed into beautiful birds who flew away to freedom.

LEGENDS GREW up around Pin Oak. After Harper's death, the house went to Mr. Kelsey at the bank, but it was destroyed by fire during the Civil War.

Olive Hill had grown up in the shadow of Pin Oak ruins. Two of the six Doric pillars and a burned-out chimney were all that was left of the stately old mansion. Whenever Papa had gone fishing, Olive liked to tag along behind him through the plantation grounds and down to Topps River Falls. There he would tell her the legend of Pin Oak.

After twenty-five years of telling it, Papa's Pin Oak story was always the same. Olive never tired of hearing it, and she had even made it the subject of a paper she was writing. For months she'd searched through old records, documents, books, and papers to see how much of the real story she could reconstruct.

The diary of Benjamin Stone, a well-known abolitionist and "conductor" on the Underground Railroad, had just been published, and it contained information she needed. When the Reader Bookstore called to tell her that her copy had arrived, she hurried over to pick it up.

Driving to the mall, Olive mentally sorted through all the details she'd uncovered about Pin Oak. Henri, a mulatto, was the son of Mary DuPriest, a free woman from New Orleans. Mary had died in 1840, and Amos had brought Henri to Pin Oak, although by law the boy was free. Years later Amos had made Henri overseer and put him in charge of Pin Oak operations—ordering, planting, harvesting, and selling crops. Henri had married Charlemae and they had had a son. It was speculated that the family had plunged to their death in Topps River Falls in a failed attempt to escape the plantation—though their bodies were never found.

Meanwhile, during the 1850s, the Underground Railroad was active in Tennessee. Through a network of conductors, runaways were led from one safe house to another, until they reached free soil.

Olive speculated that Henri might have made contact with Benjamin Stone. Conductors sometimes used old spirituals like "Steal Away" to send a signal that an escape was being planned.

A cave located behind Topps River Falls was a well-known hiding place used by the Underground Railroad. Stone no doubt knew about it and might have told Henri the night before the planned escape. Perhaps Henri and Charlemae tried to make it appear as though they jumped to their death while actually leaping to a hidden ledge and crawling to safety in the cave. Stone could have then led them to the next station and finally to freedom.

This explanation for the missing bodies seemed plausible to Olive, and she hurried home as soon as she bought the book to see if the facts supported her theory. As soon as she walked in the door, she threw off her coat and dropped it in the middle of the floor. Excitement made her hands shake as she flipped the pages of her book, looking for relevant dates, names, and places. "Pin Oak! Here it is!"

As the last rays of sunlight filtered through the window, Olive turned on the lamp beside her chair and curled up with Benjamin Stone's diary. He wrote:

> I only lost two—no, three—lives as a conductor. They were a family. The man's name was Henri from Pin Oak Plantation. I was supposed to meet him in the woods, but for some reason we missed each other. I never got to tell him about the cave behind the falls . . .

We Organized

During the Great Depression of the 1930s, government agencies sponsored programs designed to put people back to work. The Library of Congress hired hundreds of unemployed writers to interview and record the life stories of former slaves. The result of the project was a ten-thousand-page typed manuscript of folk histories, vividly retold by African Americans who had lived under the tyranny of slavery. The personal accounts in the collection, known simply as *The Slave Narratives*, are sometimes humorous, sometimes angry, and sometimes chillingly mysterious. The following poem is based on an actual slave narrative.

YOU ASK how we all got free 'fore
President Lincoln signed the paper?
Write this what I tell you.

I, Ajax,
Massa's driver . . .
I, Ajax,
Master of the whip . . . Got power!
Hear it crack! Hear it pop!
Can pluck a rose off its stem,
Never once disturbing a petal.
I can snap a moth in two
While it's still on the wing,
Pick a fly off a mule's ear
And never ruffle a hair.
One day Massa say,
"Ajax, see that hornets' nest over there?
Snatch it off that tree."
I say, "Naw sir. Not that I can't do it.
But some things just ain' wise to do."
Massa ask,
"Why not?"
I come back with,
"Them hornets be trouble.
They organized."

Tried to warn ol' Massa,
But he never once listen.
He a poor man . . . marry money.
Money prove him a fool. A mean fool.

Massa turned out Pappy Sims;
Say he too old to pick cotton.
No more use.

Be careful, Massa!
Beat Lilly Mae;
Say she too lazy to breathe.
Have mercy, Massa!
Sell Sally 'way from her husband, Lee;
See her no more.
Watch out, Massa!
Slap cook—
No reason, just wanted to and did!
Then Massa bring trouble to his own front door.
He make a promise to free Corbella, the Congo Woman.
He not do it.
Big mistake, Massa.

Just wouldn't heed a warning.
So when the lilacs bloomed,
Massa be missing a button off his coat . . . never mind.
Huh!

Deep in the night,
Hear the music, long refrain.
Dancing, chanting,
Digging a grave with words . . .
Old words . . .
Powerful words.
We pin Massa's black button to a straw doll.
Hang it in a sycamore tree.
Spinning, clapping,
Calling the names of the ancestors . . .
Old names . . .

Powerful names.
Three days dancing in the dark.
Three days chanting till dawn.

Way in the night Massa hear the music in his head.
He hear the whispered words
In a long refrain . . . and he come screaming.
"Lawd! Lawd!"
But it's too late.
Come harvest-time Massa be low sick.
Near 'bout wasted away.
All the mean gone out of him.

Massa call all us to him.
He free the Congo Woman.
He free everybody—glad to be rid of us!
Wrote out the free papers, right now!

Then he turn to me.
He say,
"Ajax, git gone!"
He didn't have to say it again.

Now, you ask me how we all got free
'Fore Massa Lincoln sign the paper?
Take heed.
Like them hornets, we organized!

Justice

The Ku Klux Klan is the most well known white supremacist organization in the country. Since its earliest beginnings, the Klan has used racial and religious intolerance to terrorize people in their homes, churches and synagogues, schools, and businesses—until recent years, with impunity. To the Klan, anybody who is *different* is automatically inferior. One of the most powerful periods for the KKK was the 1930s. Klansmen, draped in white robes and hoods, meted out horrific punishments for so-called crimes that sometimes amounted to no more than "sassing" or "being uppity." But a nineteenth-century poet and editor, William Cullen Bryant, gave a warning to all those who would make a mockery of justice: "Truth crushed to earth will rise again." You can count on it.

RILEY HOLT, the richest and most powerful man in Tallahatchie County, Mississippi, was attacked and left for dead along State Highway 49. The whole state prayed for Holt's recovery, but he died several days later, never regaining consciousness.

Nobody could remember a murder ever taking place in Tyre, unless you count Miz Jasper's cat Sidney many years earlier. Folk didn't know quite what to say or do about a real homicide.

The mayor, who was a pallbearer at Holt's funeral, announced his personal outrage at the violence perpetrated against "one of Mississippi's finest families." Holt's weeping, red-faced widow stood on the steps of the First Baptist Church and wailed for justice. The governor consoled the widow. "Don't you worry none, Miz Holt. The truth will come out. You can count on it."

Meanwhile, the burden of the investigation was dropped into the lap of Chief Burton Baker and his four-man Tyre police department. He decided to question Hoop Granger, whose filling station was near the Holt estate. Maybe he'd seen something.

Hoop Granger sat by the dirt-streaked window and watched Chief Baker walk toward Simm's Ironwork Shop, where Hoop and the other local riffraff hung out. Hoop, who'd been a difficult child, was a downright ornery man. He'd grown up bitter as quinine and meaner than a swamp snake. He made a living as a self-taught auto mechanic, having inherited the service station out on Highway 49 from his father.

Hoop warned his friends that Baker was coming. The men greeted the officer coolly.

"Like to ask you a few questions, Hoop," Baker announced.

"I'm wondering, Chief, why you wasting time talking to me, when you ought to be over in the Corners arresting one of them darkies for murdering Holt."

"Why are you jumping on the defensive?" Baker was obviously annoyed. "I came to find out if you saw something."

Hoop turned to the window. "I might have."

"Hoop, if you know anything, you'd better tell me now. Did you see somebody from the Corners out at the Holt place?"

"I seen Alvin . . ." Hoop swallowed hard. His eyes darted around, never making eye contact. "Alvin Tinsley. Yeah. He went up to Holt's on the day of the murder."

Alvin Tinsley was a young black man who was respected by both the white and black communities. He'd grown up in Tyre, and after working his way through Tuskegee Institute in veterinary science, he'd come back home. But the state of Mississippi had denied him a veterinary license. Then Alvin saved one of Riley Holt's prize walking horses, and the powerful Holt made sure Alvin got his license. Holt immediately hired Alvin to take care of all the animals on the Holt plantation.

Chief Baker looked around. Hoop's friends were nodding their heads in agreement.

"Hoop, come on over to the station and we'll talk more," he said. He opened the door, then added, "I'm going to send for Alvin. We can get to the bottom of this right now."

On his way out, Hoop turned to the chief. "You know the road leading up to the Holt place goes right by my station, so I see everything. And I swear I saw Alvin go by—looking mad enough to kill."

HALF AN HOUR later Alvin Tinsley was shown into the chief's office. Politely removing his hat, he took the seat Chief Baker offered him. Hoop shifted uneasily in his chair as he watched a black man being given the same courtesy as a white.

His mind went back twenty years when he and Alvin had sat in this same office. He remembered accusing Alvin of another crime—of hanging Miz Jasper's cat. And he remembered Alvin admitting that he'd done it . . . just as Hoop had made him do. "If you don't say you did it, I'll tell my daddy to fire your daddy, then he won't have no job."

Hoop still remembered Chief Baker's eyes staring at him. "Are you sure this is what happened?" he'd said.

"Sure, Chief," Hoop had answered. "It was just like I said. Alvin killed that dumb ol' cat for scratching him, but he's sorry."

"It's strange to me . . . the only one who's got scratches on his hand is you, Hoop."

But Alvin had held to Hoop's story and taken the punishment without complaint.

Now here they were again, sitting before Chief Baker.

"Seems like we've done this before," Baker said, sighing. "How's Miz Cora Mae?" he asked, putting off official business. Then, "Alvin, can you tell me about your movements on or around the thirteenth of June 1938 . . . ? That was last Thursday."

"Mama's doing nicely," Alvin said, answering the chief's first question. "I was over in Mound Bayou," he said, answering the second one. "Left Wednesday evening. My mother-in-law is sick, so my wife and I took the bus over to see about her. Is there a reason why you're asking?" Alvin looked at Hoop with troubled eyes.

"That'd give you a good alibi, and it's easy enough to check," the chief said, immediately dispatching Officer Peterson over to the hardware store that doubled as a bus station to verify Alvin's story.

"Why do I need an alibi?" Alvin was surprised.

"Hoop here says he saw you arguing with Mr. Holt on the thirteenth. Is that true?"

Alvin turned to Hoop. "Not this time you don't," he said. And turning back to Chief Baker, "No sir. Sure, I was out to the Holt place last Wednesday before I left. He sent for me. Wanted me to go up to Memphis with him to look at a filly when I got back. But not one cross word passed between us."

"You saying I'm a liar?"

Alvin sighed. "I'm not calling you a liar. I'm saying I'm telling the truth."

The men sat in stony silence until Peterson came in and handed a note to Chief Baker.

"Well, Alvin, seems your story holds up. You see this, Hoop? Presley over at the store says he sold Alvin and Opal a ticket on the twelfth from here to Mound Bayou." The chief stood and extended his hand, which Alvin shook. "You may go. Sorry we had to put you through all this, but for the record I had to ask. Tell Miz Cora Mae I'll be over for a slice of sweet potato pie first chance I get."

"I'll tell her you asked about her," Alvin said, glancing at Hoop before leaving.

Hoop slammed his fist into his palm. "You letting him go? I can't believe you taking that darky's word over *mine*."

"Alvin didn't call you a liar," Chief Baker snapped at Hoop. "You and them shop boys got the coloreds around here scared to death of you. But I'm not. You're lying out of your teeth, and I hate to think why." The chief leaned over his desk and forced the man to make eye contact. "Where were you last Thursday?"

Hoop looked at his feet. "Working at my station pumping gas. Got witnesses aplenty. Ask Jake, Bo, and Tomie Lee."

Chief Baker turned in his swivel chair. With his back to Hoop, he said, "Why, I'd have to be possessed by a clown to believe a word that fell out of any one of your mouths. Now git, and make sure that bald-faced lie you hatched about Alvin dies quickly."

But the chief's warning didn't do a thing to stop Hoop. Back at the ironwork shop he told his buddies, "Alvin killed Holt, and I know it." He sauntered over to the cooler and pulled out a cold drink, putting a nickel in the cup on the counter. He straddled a chair and leaned back against the wall. "I told Baker-boy what I seen, and what did he do? He insulted me, laughed at me in front of that uppity nigger passing hisself off as some kinda horse doctor with a fancy name!"

Anger fueled Hoop's speech. "A white man's life was taken right here in our town. Who's next . . . our wives, daughters, mothers? And what does the chief of police do? I'll tell you! He shakes the murderer's hand like they was equals. That shows Baker ain't gonna do nothing." He spat as if he had a bad taste in his mouth. "I says it's time we take charge. Like the Bible says. 'An eye for an eye and a tooth for a tooth.' "

It didn't take much to convince the rowdy gang at Simm's that an innocent man was guilty. "Are we gon' suffer a murdering black coon to walk among us unpunished?" Hoop asked in conclusion.

A silent signal passed from man to man. In groups of two or three they left.

HOOP LOVED the white robe of a Klansman. Wearing it made him feel powerful and strong—even safe. He pulled the hood over his head and hurried out the door. A passing pickup slowed down just long enough for him to jump aboard.

Seven cars and trucks roared down Russell Avenue at twelve thirty A.M. By two thirty in the morning the Ku Klux Klan had dragged Alvin from his house and taken him to a clearing down by the Tallahatchie River. There, under a Mississippi blood moon with a flaming cross of fire, they tried, convicted, and sentenced him for the murder of Riley Holt.

"You ain't so uppity now, are you? You not so important now that Holt ain't here to protect you," Hoop mocked Alvin. "If you looking for somebody to blame for what's happening now, blame that nigger school that made you think you could get out of your place, boy."

Hoop darted around in the glowing firelight. "This is the guilty one, all right. Make no mistake about that." Then, turning to the condemned man, he said, "Why don't you admit you did it, boy? Say you're guilty. Say it!" A Klansman put the rope around Alvin's neck.

Precious in the sight of the Lord is the death of his saints. Alvin mumbled psalms of comfort he'd learned as a child. His eyes had been beaten shut. He struggled to speak. "You can't make me confess to a crime I didn't commit . . . again," he said, agony twisting his face. "I'm innocent. And I'm going to prove it!"

Hoop stopped laughing. He moved in close to torment his victim. "You gonna be dead. And dead men can't do nothing!"

Alvin managed to whisper a last promise. "I'm coming back. Watch for me!"

"You threatening me?" Hoop raised his voice in mock rage but felt very much in control. Then he kicked the stump from underneath Alvin, snapping the man's neck instantly.

THE NEXT DAY the mayor released a ludicrous report: Alvin Tinsley had hanged himself after confessing to Riley Holt's murder. All the good citizens of Tyre publicly accepted the report—whether they believed it or not—satisfied that the untidy mess had been cleared up and life could go back to normal.

Alvin's widow and mother claimed his body at the morgue in the courthouse basement. The authorities had his coffin officially sealed so none of his family or friends ever got to see his body. The day after they buried Alvin, his widow left for Chicago. Those who stayed in Tyre knew that Alvin's death hadn't solved Riley Holt's murder. But they felt helpless to do anything about it. They accepted his murder as "the way things are," and for them, life went back to normal, too.

But for Hoop Granger life would never be the same.

AT FIRST Hoop reveled in knowing he'd finally presided over a Klan lynching, savoring the excitement and power he felt. He'd carried himself well in front of the others. Why, he might even run for Grand Imperial Wizard, or maybe for mayor next election. He had a good chance, knowing what he knew about certain prominent citizens.

But at the height of his exhilaration Hoop began having nightmares. In his dreams he'd be getting ready for bed when Alvin's raspy voice would whisper into the darkness, *I'm coming back . . . back . . . back!*

Hoop would jerk himself awake with a scream caught in his throat, then lie staring into space, unable to fall asleep again, sometimes too frightened to try. During the day, he was restless and nervous, too tired to focus on the simplest chores. He was testy with his customers and impatient with his friends, who'd started to distance themselves from him. Still the dreams relentlessly returned each night.

One morning about two weeks after Alvin had been buried, Hoop woke up panting for breath and soaked in sweat. He hadn't been dreaming . . . or had he? Nothing was clear anymore. It didn't matter, because it was daylight. He could get up, maybe open the station. Where were the keys? It was so hard to remember lately.

That's when he saw the curious hazy substance on every windowpane in his bedroom. *Watch for me. Watch for me.* The film covered every window in his house. Even though Hoop wasn't much on housekeeping, he had to admit his windows needed washing. He cleaned them inside and out until they shined crystal clear.

The following morning he slept until ten o'clock, something he hadn't been able to do in weeks. It was his first sound night of sleep since the lynching. He felt better.

Stumbling groggily into the kitchen, Hoop fixed himself a cup of coffee. That's when he noticed the windows were cloudy again. Looking closer, he saw images taking shape on the panes, slowly developing like photo negatives. *Coming back . . . coming back . . .*

Quickly Hoop made a strong mixture of ammonia water and scrubbed the windows feverishly. He worked until after noon, completely forgetting to open the station again.

Bo, one of Hoop's drinking buddies and fellow Klansmen, stopped by. "You sick or something? You ain't been down to Simm's in over a week. Hey, I came by yesterday and the place looked deserted. You open for business today?"

"Pump your own gas. Leave me alone — can't you see I'm busy?" Hoop pushed Bo away.

"Those windows are sparkling like new money. Why you keep wiping?"

"Can't you see that—that gunk on 'em?"

Bo looked. "Where? I don't see nothing."

"Get out of here!" Hoop shouted angrily. "Go on, get out!"

"It's right what everybody's been saying," Bo said, backing toward his pickup. "You have gone loony."

Hoop flashed Bo an angry glance. "What do folks know?" he said suspiciously. "What have you been telling them about me, Bo?

I can have you punished for running your mouth too much."

"I ain't said a thing to nobody," Bo said, and turned to leave.

Hoop dismissed him with a wave of his hand and went back to his work. But as hard as he tried, he couldn't stop the images from forming. He groaned when he saw the outline of a dead cat hanging from a tree and the outline of a boy standing beside it. "No, no!" he shouted, recognizing the scene from his past.

"It's Alvin! It's Alvin!" Hoop pleaded with the chief. "He ain't dead. He's come back and is deviling me . . . doing stuff."

"Now why would Alvin choose to devil you?" Baker chuckled sarcastically.

"Because." Silence. Hoop looked at his feet.

Chief Baker grabbed Hoop by the collar. "I know that you and them Kluxer maniacs lynched Alvin Tinsley, who had nothing to do with Holt's murder. But what's worse is that I ended up being forced to cover for the lot of you just to save the mayor's boy, who was out there with y'all. But it's not over. Alvin didn't kill Holt. The whole thing sticks in my throat like a fish bone, and I've got to hawk it up or choke to death on it. You get my meaning?" Chief Baker released his hold on Hoop.

"Alvin ain't dead. He's back."

"Oh, I assure you Alvin is very dead. I saw what you did to that poor man. But if the grave has delivered him up to torment you, he's got my eternal blessing. Now get out of here. You sicken me!"

Hoop staggered out of the police station, dreading what awaited him at home.

Even though he could ill afford to lose the income, he closed the station and spent the rest of the day trying to stop the pictures. But they just kept getting clearer and clearer. Although the facial details were not filled in, Hoop knew what each scene would show.

Starting in the living room, Hoop saw a car sitting on the side of a road. There were two men arguing. He closed his eyes, remembering. The back bedroom window showed a man holding out a piece of paper. Then he saw a man hitting another one with a rock. On the kitchen window was a man running down the road. And etched on the back-door window was the frightful dead face of a hanged man with accusing dark eyes.

Frantically Hoop picked up a hammer and tried to shatter the glass in the windows. It cracked but somehow held in place. He tried boarding up the windows, but the nails popped out. He drenched the house with gasoline and threw a match to it, but the fire fizzled, then died. In fact, no matter what Hoop tried, the truth about what he'd done remained etched in the glass. On the seventh day after the images first appeared, the pictures were completely developed and framed like a bizarre photo gallery. Then came the sounds. As he stood in front of the window showing the two men arguing, Hoop heard the sound of his own voice.

"I'll pay back every penny I owe you as soon as business picks up. You know how hard times are."

He heard Holt's answer exactly as he had said it. "Sorry, Hoop, but times are hard for everybody, even me. I've been fair, given you countless extensions. But you haven't even tried to make regular payments. Alvin Tinsley borrowed money from me, and he paid me back every penny and on time. If he can do it, then you can certainly do better."

"Don't compare me to no nigger," Hoop heard himself say angrily. Even now he could feel the fury that had raged inside him.

"I didn't," Holt retorted. "There couldn't possibly be a comparison between the two of you. Now will you sign this quitclaim deed or not?" It was clear that Holt had run out of patience.

"No. I can't lose my station. It was my daddy's, and it's all I've got."

"You may work and live there same as now. You may keep what you earn, less my share, which will be ten percent. I can't be any fairer."

Hoop moved to the next window, where Riley Holt was walking back to his car. "You helped that nigger get on his feet, but you won't give me a chance!" he shouted. Holt shook his head in disgust. Then Hoop saw himself hit the man from behind with a rock, take the paper, and run away. "I didn't mean to kill you, Mr. Holt," Hoop pleaded with the image.

"But you meant to kill *me!*" Hoop whirled around. He fell against the back wall, his mouth open in horror, his eyes frozen in fear. On the back-door window Alvin's hideously bloated face grimaced as it spoke. *"I'm back!"*

THAT SAME evening, Hoop bolted into the police station and melted into a hysterical heap of sobbing misery. Confession poured out of him. "Make him stop! Make him stop! I admit it, I killed Mr. Holt. I killed Alvin. Now make the pictures on the windows go away."

"Only you can make the pictures go away," Chief Baker said. Then he silently gave Peterson a signal to have a patrol car go by Hoop's place.

"Alvin said he was coming back," Hoop groaned. "And he did."

"What did Alvin come back for?"

"Revenge?"

"Try justice."

Seconds after Hoop signed a full confession, an officer radioed from his patrol car that Hoop's station and adjoining house had exploded in fire, shattering every window in the place.

The 11:59

From 1880 to 1960—a time known as the golden age of train travel—George Pullman's luxury sleeping cars provided passengers with comfortable accommodations during an overnight trip. The men who changed the riding seats into well-made-up beds and attended to the individual needs of each passenger were called Pullman car porters. For decades all the porters were African Americans, so when they organized the Brotherhood of Sleeping Car Porters in 1926, theirs was the first all-black union in the United States. Like most groups, the porters had their own language and a network of stories. The phantom Death Train, known in railroad language as the 11:59, is an example of the kind of story the porters often shared.

LESTER SIMMONS was a thirty-year retired Pullman car porter—had his gold watch to prove it. "Keeps perfect train time," he often bragged. "Good to the second."

Daily he went down to the St. Louis Union Station and shined shoes to help supplement his meager twenty-four-dollar-a-month Pullman retirement check. He ate his evening meal at the porter house on Compton Avenue and hung around until late at night talking union, playing bid whist, and spinning yarns with those who were still "travelin' men." In this way Lester stayed in touch with the only family he'd known since 1920.

There was nothing the young porters liked more than listening to Lester tell true stories about the old days, during the founding of the Brotherhood of Sleeping Car Porters, the first black union in the United States. He knew the president, A. Philip Randolph, personally, and proudly boasted that it was Randolph who'd signed him up as a union man back in 1926. He passed his original card around for inspection. "I knew all the founding brothers. Take Brother E. J. Bradley. We hunted many a day together, not for the sport of it but for something to eat. Those were hard times, starting up the union. But we hung in there so you youngsters might have the benefits you enjoy now."

The rookie porters always liked hearing about the thirteen-year struggle between the Brotherhood and the powerful Pullman Company, and how, against all odds, the fledgling union had won recognition and better working conditions.

Everybody enjoyed it too when Lester told tall tales about Daddy Joe, the porters' larger-than-life hero. "Now y'all know the first thing a good Pullman man is expected to do is make up the top and lower berths for the passengers each night."

"Come on, Lester," one of his listeners chided. "You don't need to describe our jobs for us."

"Some of you, maybe not. But some of you, well—" he said, looking over the top of his glasses and raising an eyebrow at a few of the younger porters. "I was just setting the stage." He smiled good-naturedly and went on with his story. "They tell me Daddy Joe could walk flatfooted down the center of the coach and let down berths on both sides of the aisle."

Hearty laughter filled the room, because everyone knew that to accomplish such a feat, Daddy Joe would have to have been superhuman. But that was it: To the men who worked the sleeping cars, Daddy Joe was no less a hero than Paul Bunyan was to the lumberjacks of the Northwestern forests.

"And when the 11:59 pulled up to his door, as big and strong as Daddy Joe was . . ." Lester continued solemnly. "Well, in the end even he couldn't escape the 11:59." The old storyteller eyed one of the rookie porters he knew had never heard the frightening tale about the porters' Death Train. Lester took joy in mesmerizing his young listeners with all the details.

"Any porter who hears the whistle of the 11:59 has got exactly twenty-four hours to clear up earthly matters. He better be ready when the train comes the next night . . ." In his creakiest voice, Lester drove home the point. "All us porters got to board that train one day. Ain't no way to escape the final ride on the 11:59."

Silence.

"Lester," a young porter asked, "you know anybody who ever heard the whistle of the 11:59 and lived to tell—"

"Not a living soul!"

Laughter.

"Well," began one of the men, "wonder will we have to make up berths on *that* train?"

"If it's an overnight trip to heaven, you can best be believing there's bound to be a few of us making up the berths," another answered.

"Shucks," a card player stopped to put in. "They say even up in heaven *we* the ones gon' be keeping all that gold and silver polished."

"Speaking of gold and silver," Lester said, remembering. "That reminds me of how I gave Tip Sampson his nickname. Y'all know Tip?"

There were plenty of nods and smiles.

The memory made Lester chuckle. He shifted in his seat to find a more comfortable spot. Then he began. "A woman got on board the *Silver Arrow* in Chicago going to Los Angeles. She was dripping in finery—had on all kinds of gold and diamond jewelry, carried twelve bags. Sampson knocked me down getting to wait on her, figuring she was sure for a big tip. That lady was worrisome! Ooo-wee! 'Come do this. Go do that. Bring me this.' Sampson was running over himself trying to keep that lady happy. When we reached L.A., my passengers all tipped me two or three dollars, as was customary back then.

"When Sampson's Big Money lady got off, she reached into her purse and placed a dime in his outstretched hand. A *dime!* Can you imagine? *Ow!* You should have seen his face. And I didn't make it no better. Never did let him forget it. I teased him so—went to calling him Tip, and the nickname stuck."

Laughter.

"I haven't heard from ol' Tip in a while. Anybody know anything?"

"You haven't got word, Lester? Tip boarded the 11:59 over in Kansas City about a month ago."

"Sorry to hear that. That just leaves me and Willie Beavers, the last of the old, old-timers here in St. Louis."

Lester looked at his watch—it was a little before midnight. The talkfest had lasted later than usual. He said his good-byes and left, taking his usual route across the Eighteenth Street bridge behind the station.

In the darkness, Lester looked over the yard, picking out familiar shapes—the *Hummingbird,* the *Zephyr.* He'd worked on them both. Train travel wasn't anything like it used to be in the old days—not since people had begun to ride airplanes. "Progress," he scoffed. "Those contraptions will never take the place of a train. No sir!"

Suddenly he felt a sharp pain in his chest. At exactly the same moment he heard the mournful sound of a train whistle, which the wind seemed to carry from some faraway place. Ignoring his pain, Lester looked at the old station. He knew nothing was scheduled to come in or out till early morning. Nervously he lit a match to check the time. 11:59!

"No," he said into the darkness. "I'm not ready. I've got plenty of living yet."

Fear quickened his step. Reaching his small apartment, he hurried up the steps. His heart pounded in his ear, and his left arm tingled. He had an idea, and there wasn't a moment to waste. But his own words haunted him. *Ain't no way to escape the final ride on the 11:59.*

"But I'm gon' try!" Lester spent the rest of the night plotting his escape from fate.

"I won't eat or drink anything all day," he talked himself through his plan. "That way I can't choke, die of food poisoning, or cause a cooking fire."

Lester shut off the space heater to avoid an explosion, nailed shut all doors and windows to keep out intruders, and unplugged every electrical appliance. Good weather was predicted, but just in case a freak storm came and blew out a window, shooting deadly glass shards in his direction, he moved a straight-backed chair into a far corner, making sure nothing was overhead to fall on him.

"I'll survive," he said, smiling at the prospect of beating Death. "Won't that be a wonderful story to tell at the porter house?" He rubbed his left arm. It felt numb again.

Lester sat silently in his chair all day, too afraid to move. At noon someone knocked on his door. He couldn't answer it. Footsteps . . . another knock. He didn't answer.

A parade of minutes passed by, equally measured, one behind the other, ticking . . . ticking . . . away . . . The dull pain in his chest returned. He nervously checked his watch every few minutes.

Ticktock, ticktock.

Time had always been on his side. Now it was his enemy. Where had the years gone? Lester reviewed the thirty years he'd spent riding the rails. How different would his life have been if he'd married Louise Henderson and had a gallon of children? What if he'd taken that job at the mill down in Opelika? What if he'd followed his brother to Philly? How different?

Ticktock, ticktock.

So much living had passed so quickly. Lester decided if he had to do it all over again, he'd stand by his choices. His had been a good life. No regrets. No major changes for him.

Ticktock, ticktock.

The times he'd had—both good and bad—what memories. His first and only love had been traveling, and she was a jealous companion. Wonder whatever happened to that girl up in Minneapolis? Thinking about her made him smile. Then he laughed. That *girl* must be close to seventy years old by now.

Ticktock, ticktock.

Daylight was fading quickly. Lester drifted off to sleep, then woke from a nightmare in which, like Jonah, he'd been swallowed by an enormous beast. Even awake he could still hear its heart beating . . . *ticktock, ticktock* . . . But then he realized he was hearing his own heartbeat.

Lester couldn't see his watch, but he guessed no more than half an hour had passed. Sleep had overtaken him with such little resistance. Would Death, that shapeless shadow, slip in that easily? Where was he lurking? *Yea, though I walk through the valley of the shadow of death, I will fear no evil* . . . The Twenty-third Psalm was the only prayer Lester knew, and he repeated it over and over, hoping it would comfort him.

Lester rubbed his tingling arm. He could hear the blood rushing past his ear and up the side of his head. He longed to know what time it was, but that meant he had to light a match—too risky. What if there was a gas leak? The match would set off an explosion. "I'm too smart for that, Death," he said.

Ticktock, ticktock.

It was late. He could feel it. Stiffness seized his legs and made them tremble. How much longer? he wondered. Was he close to winning?

Then in the fearful silence he heard a train whistle. His ears strained to identify the sound, making sure it *was* a whistle. No mistake. It came again, the same as the night before. Lester answered it with a groan.

Ticktock, ticktock.

He could hear Time ticking away in his head. Gas leak or not, he had to see his watch. Striking a match, Lester quickly checked the time. 11:57.

Although there was no gas explosion, a tiny explosion erupted in his heart.

Ticktock, ticktock.

Just a little more time. The whistle sounded again. Closer than before. Lester struggled to move, but he felt fastened to the chair. Now he could hear the engine puffing, pulling a heavy load. It was hard for him to breathe, too, and the pain in his chest weighed heavier and heavier.

Ticktock, ticktock.

Time had run out! Lester's mind reached for an explanation that made sense. But reason failed when a glowing phantom dressed in the porters' blue uniform stepped out of the grayness of Lester's confusion.

"It's *your* time, good brother." The specter spoke in a thousand familiar voices.

Freed of any restraint now, Lester stood, bathed in a peaceful calm that had its own glow. "Is that you, Tip?" he asked, squinting to focus on his old friend standing in the strange light.

"It's me, ol' partner. Come to remind you that none of us can escape the last ride on the 11:59."

"I know. I know," Lester said, chuckling. "But man, I had to try."

Tip smiled. "I can dig it. So did I."

"That'll just leave Willie, won't it?"

"Not for long."

"I'm ready."

Lester saw the great beam of the single headlight and heard the deafening whistle blast one last time before the engine tore through the front of the apartment, shattering glass and splintering wood, collapsing everything in its path, including Lester's heart.

WHEN LESTER didn't show up at the shoeshine stand two days running, friends went over to his place and found him on the floor. His eyes were fixed on something quite amazing—his gold watch, stopped at exactly 11:59.

The Sight

Until recent years, midwives attended almost all women during childbirth. One of the midwife's many duties was to tell mothers when their babies were born with the caul, a filmy part of the amnion, covering their faces. Those special children were said to have psychic abilities. It was called being born with a veil, and the powers were called the sight. If the mother was a believer, the midwife usually explained the ways of the sight: Many never got the power, but for those who did, it could be both a blessing and a curse.

"YOUR BABY'S been born with a veil over his face," the midwife told Amanda Mayes. "Are you a believer?"

Amanda nodded.

"He may have the sight."

Worry lines creased the new mother's forehead as the woman explained. "The sight comes—if it comes—in different ways. Some can see spirits, while others can see the future or can divine. Make sure he uses it wisely, or it will bring trouble."

THE SIGHT would come to Esau at two times in his life—the first when he was only six years old.

Esau and his mother lived on a small farm outside St. Charles, Missouri, where Amanda scratched out a living doing laundry. One Friday evening the boy told his mother matter-of-factly, "Miz Toppy won't be to church on Sunday 'cause she's going to break her leg." Sure enough, Saturday evening Toppy Perkins slipped on a patch of freshly cut grass and broke her leg.

From that day on the sight was strong with Esau. It gave him the gift to see the future with incredible accuracy. In the beginning he was an open vessel through which psychic energy flowed, overwhelmed by mental images that showed him things he didn't want to know. But as he grew older he learned how to manage the visions better, controlling them with his mind.

Fearing people might misuse the boy, Amanda taught her son to keep his gift hidden deep inside him. "You must be careful who you choose to tell about the sight," she warned. "Certain folk might tempt you to use it for the wrong reasons. And if you do, the sight will leave you for sure." So Esau never told another soul—until his pa showed up.

There wasn't a worse husband or more neglectful father than Tall Mayes. But he was charming and able to con the devil's best man out of his shoes. Tall had left St. Charles right after Esau's birth, coming back only two or three times, begging for forgiveness and making big promises. Then as unexpectedly as he'd come Tall would leave.

"Trouble's comin' to our door," Esau told his mother one August morning. Tall Mayes showed up three days later on the boy's ninth birthday.

"Hide the silver," Amanda said sarcastically. "Your pa is home!"

Tall drove right up to the front porch in a shiny new 1931 Ford, kicking up dust and scattering the hens and chicks every which way. He leaped out, bearing gifts of candy, flowers, toys, and lots of talk, most of it apologies for not being around for the past year.

"Now, Amanda, you know I love you and the boy," he said, flashing a quick smile. "I admit I'm a rascal, but this time I'm home for good. My roaming days are over."

Liar, Esau thought.

As disgusted as Amanda acted and as reluctant as Esau was to warm up to him, within the hour Tall had them dancing and laughing and turning like puppets on a string. Esau couldn't recall a happier birthday.

A week later Esau went into St. Charles with his father. When Tall left for a moment to make a telephone call, the boy had a vision. As soon as Tall came back to the car, Esau blurted out, "Those men you owe money to? They're coming to hurt you bad, Pa. Real bad!"

"How did you know about . . . ?" his father screamed. Right away Esau knew he'd made a mistake by speaking up. But what else could he have done? He had to warn his father.

Then in a flash Tall's mood lightened. He slapped his thigh and clapped his hands as he remembered. "Ain't this a blessing! I knew you were born with a veil over your face, but I thought that was just old wives' tales." He laughed. "Amanda sure kept this a secret. Tell me, son, do you really have the gift?"

Reluctantly Esau nodded but quickly added, "Ma says I shouldn't use it to do wrong, because I'll lose it."

Tall exaggerated a look of surprise. "I wouldn't dream of making you do anything wrong." But Esau knew better.

As soon as they got home Tall started packing. Amanda had left a note saying she had gone to visit the sick and shut-in with Elder and Mrs. Lampkin. She wasn't expected home for another hour or so.

"You're comin' with me, boy," Tall announced. "Time I had some influence in your life."

"What about Ma? I don't want to go without her." Tall ignored the boy's protests, and Esau started to panic. "No," he cried. "I won't go!"

"Yes, you will," Tall said, throwing the boy's things into the trunk of the car. "Not to worry. Your ma knows I'm taking you. I told her last night and she agreed." Tall forced Esau inside the car. "That's why she left home. You know how much she hates good-byes."

Esau knew his father was lying. His mother wouldn't agree to such a thing. "I don't want to go!" he screamed as Tall stepped on the gas and tore out of the driveway and down the dirt road.

ONE MONTH LATER Tall dropped Esau off at the front gate and sped out of their lives for good. Amanda listened silently while her son recounted how he'd helped Tall win big money by using the sight to pick winning numbers and horses. "He made enough to pay back the bad men, but he wouldn't stop gambling."

Esau's voice grew quieter. "Then something happened," he went on. "Pa made me call on the sight to pick a horse. But this time I couldn't see a thing. Pa beat me and beat me until I finally chose one."

Amanda clicked her teeth and shook her head sadly.

Esau continued his story. "Pa bet on that horse and lost every penny. When the bad men caught up with us, he couldn't pay them. He made promises and even told them about my gift, but they laughed at him. Then they punched him around . . . just like I saw that they would."

"None of it's your fault," Amanda said, hugging him up close.

"Since then I haven't had the sight anymore. I call to it, but it doesn't come."

"Maybe you're better off without it."

Losing the sight didn't matter much to Esau either. He didn't like knowing a friend or a family member was in trouble anyway.

And as he grew up, Esau forgot that he'd ever had the sight to begin with.

A LOT OF Missouri boys saw action in World War II, and among them was Esau Mayes. Esau was one of the lucky ones who made it back healthy and whole, and with a wife, too. He'd met Charity Rose in St. Louis while on furlough after his training at Fort Leonard Wood. "The first night we met it was like we had known each other all our lives," Esau told Amanda the day he brought his new wife home to River Ridge.

Soon after the twins were born, Amanda gave the farm to Esau and Charity Rose, and she moved into a small house in town. The city girl took to country ways easily, and there wasn't a more loving husband or kinder father than Esau. "Somewhere there is a man who is as happy as me," Esau said, saluting Charity Rose at their tenth-anniversary party, "but no man can claim to be happier."

But as soon as the words had passed his mouth, he felt uneasy. That night Esau had a nightmare. It frightened him so much he couldn't go back to sleep. The next night he had the same dream. After splashing his face with cold water, he checked on the boys and crawled back into bed. Again he was afraid to sleep for fear the dream would return.

Still the dream came night after night. It always began with the smell of oil. Then he saw smoke, black billowing smoke. Next came the heat. As Esau lay trapped in a dream state, he was forced to watch his family being swallowed up by a wall of hissing flames.

His eyes were closed, but still he experienced it all. *He felt himself running, running . . . pain clawed at his leg . . . more heat, choking smoke. His head thrashed from side to side searching for his children, who called, "Daddy! Daddy! Over here!" More running. A shadowy figure holding him back. Charity Rose screaming "No, no, no!" Fire! Water! Smoke! Screams! Then a powerful force snatching him, jerking him, slamming him against the ground.*

Esau's eyes snapped open. Gasping for breath, he lay engulfed in his own fear.

Even though he desperately wanted to believe it meant nothing, Esau knew his dream was more than a nightmare. The sight had returned.

Not wanting to frighten Charity Rose or the boys, Esau kept the dreams to himself. It was the first time he'd ever had a secret from his wife, and she sensed something was wrong. When Esau brought home a new oil heater to replace the one they'd just bought a year earlier, she asked him what was the matter.

"I'm okay," he assured her. "I haven't been sleeping well." That was as much of the truth as he dared tell. "Just need some rest, that's all."

Charity Rose didn't probe, and he was grateful. Besides, the dreams stopped. After a week had passed, Esau was convinced that the old oil heater had been the problem and that replacing it had offset the impending disaster. He let himself relax.

Then one morning while he was working in the barn Esau smelled smoke. Looking around to see what might be burning, he realized the sight was upon him.

Esau knew he wasn't dreaming—he was wide awake. As he fought to free himself from the paralyzing trance, his body trembled in convulsive jerks. Choking on smoke, he felt the heat, saw the explosion and fire, heard the screams.

Esau also heard Charity Rose calling his name, but he couldn't answer. Then slowly the sight let go its grip. He was soaking wet, cold and shivering, coughing, and sore. Beside him was his wife, wiping his face with a cool cloth.

There was no way for him to keep his secret any longer. Esau told Charity Rose everything. "I was born with this curse," he said, pacing the floor as he talked. "I can see things that are going to happen in the future. It's called having the sight."

"Amanda told me about your special gift, but I thought it was just a story."

"It sounds crazy, I know. But it's true. You and the boys are in danger—real danger!"

Fear darkened Charity Rose's face. "Could you be wrong?"

Hugging her tightly, Esau continued. "No. Even though it's hard, please believe me. This fire's going to happen. Trust me."

"I trust you, Esau. Now what should we do?"

He managed to smile. With Charity Rose's support, Esau felt as if he'd set up his first line of defense. "I'll take you and the boys to Ma's house for a few days. You'll be safe there."

"No. Let's take the boys, then you and I can come back and

face whatever is going to happen the way we always have—together."

"Listen," Esau said firmly. "I have a plan, but you've got to let me stay here alone."

Charity Rose hesitated but finally agreed. Esau was relieved. He rushed on with his idea. "So far I've been resisting the sight. If I know you're safe, I'll open up to it and maybe some of the shadowy details will become clearer."

It was settled then. Esau would stay at the farm. "Promise me you won't use that oil stove no matter how cold it gets," said Charity Rose.

When the boys came home from school, Esau drove his family to his mother's house. "The sight has come back," he told her, then returned to the farm right away, leaving Charity Rose to fill in the details.

The sun had set, but there was still enough daylight to finish his evening chores. Afterward he fixed himself a sandwich and ate in silence. The house was chilly, so he wrapped himself in a quilt and sat by the fireplace. The November wind shook the latches.

As he sat staring into the fire Esau did something he hadn't done since childhood. He opened his mind to the sight. And it came.

Now Esau was inside a house. He knew it well—the mantel with the crystal candlesticks and his military photo. Lower down, the wine-colored couch and matching chair. On the table, a pair of glasses and a newspaper. Suddenly the smell of smoke. An old oil heater growing hotter and hotter, overheating, getting ready to explode. Back to the newspaper. His mind's eye racing over the date: November 14, 1954. Today!

With all his strength Esau forced himself out of the trance. Still the sight held his mind.

The oil heater blazing brighter and brighter. The furniture growing even clearer. Why, this wasn't his own farm at all! This was his mother's house!

"Nooooo!" he screamed.

Blindly racing outside, Esau prayed it wouldn't be too late. He fumbled in the darkness for the keys that were always in the ignition, then panicked. They weren't there. No time to waste looking. He hot-wired the truck and roared up the drive and onto the county road.

The psychic bombardment continued, clearer than it had ever been before. He saw puffs of oily smoke escape from the heater. Down the hall his mother and Charity Rose slept soundly in the front bedroom. The boys were in the back room. How he wanted to be there to pick them up and carry them to safety.

"Charity Rose!" he called out with his mind. "Wake up, honey. Get the children and Ma. Get out of that house. *Now!*"

Esau pushed down on the accelerator as he passed the five-mile marker. The truck swerved to miss an oncoming car. "Charity Rose, wake up! Get out of that house! Get out of that house!" he called again and again.

When the oil heater exploded, Esau saw it. The mental flash blinded him and he lost control of the truck. It skidded off the road and crashed into a ditch. Although he was unconscious only a few minutes, he felt as if he'd been out for hours.

Pulling himself from the wreckage, Esau screamed. He'd cut his leg in the accident and the gash was spouting blood. He ripped a sleeve out of his shirt and tied it around the wound. The pain was severe, but he ignored it and stumbled toward the orange glow on the horizon. He heard sirens in the distance and saw flashing lights.

When Esau turned down Carpenter Street, he saw volunteer fire fighters with hoses doing what they could to contain the fire.

Esau stumbled onto the scene like a miscued actor. Turning in confusion, he ran toward the flaming house. The heat and smoke choked him and his leg hurt, but still he kept running.

"Daddy! Daddy! Over here!" his children screamed. The smoke billowed out of the broken windows. Esau tried to run, but someone was holding him back—one of the firemen. Strengthened by a burst of adrenaline, he wrestled himself free and continued to charge.

"No! No! No!" he heard Charity Rose yell.

A wall of flames towered in front of him. The heat was intense. Suddenly he felt himself being violently pushed, jerked, and slammed against the ground, rolling and tumbling like a rag doll. He collapsed in anguish.

WHEN ESAU came around, it was just as he'd seen in the vision; he was cold and shivering, coughing, and sore. But he was surrounded by his family. Charity Rose had covered him with a warm, dry blanket.

"Sorry I had to turn the hose on you, Esau," said one of the firemen. "That was the only way to stop you from going inside."

"I thought my family was—"

"We were over here, Daddy," one of his sons said. "Didn't you hear us calling?"

"The sight proved to be a blessing to us," Amanda comforted him. "We're safe. We're safe. You saved us."

"Yes, we're okay," Charity Rose said, hugging Esau. "We got out before the explosion. I heard you."

The Woman in the Snow

The year-long Montgomery, Alabama, bus boycott in 1955–56 was a pivotal event in the American civil rights movement. Blacks refused to ride the buses until their demand of fair and equal treatment for all fare-paying passengers was met. Today the right to sit anywhere on a public bus may seem a small victory over racism and discrimination. But that single issue changed the lives of African Americans everywhere. After the successful boycott in Montgomery, blacks in other cities challenged bus companies, demanding not only the right to sit wherever they chose but also employment opportunities for black bus drivers. Many cities had their own "bus" stories. Some are in history books, but this story is best enjoyed by the fireplace on the night of the first snowfall.

GRADY BISHOP had just been hired as a driver for Metro Bus Service. When he put on the gray uniform and boarded his bus, nothing mattered, not his obesity, not his poor education, not growing up the eleventh child of the town drunk. Driving gave him power. And power mattered.

One cold November afternoon Grady clocked in for the three-to-eleven shift. "You've got Hall tonight," Billy, the route manager, said matter-of-factly.

"The Blackbird Express." Grady didn't care who knew about his nickname for the route. "Not again." He turned around, slapping his hat against his leg.

"Try the *Hall Street Express,*" Billy corrected Grady, then hurried on, cutting their conversation short. "Snow's predicted. Try to keep on schedule, but if it gets too bad out there, forget it. Come on in."

Grady popped a fresh stick of gum into his mouth. "You're the boss. But tell me. How am I s'posed to stay on schedule? What do those people care about time?"

Most Metro drivers didn't like the Hall Street assignment in the best weather, because the road twisted and turned back on itself like a retreating snake. When slick with ice and snow, it was even more hazardous. But Grady had his own reason for hating the route. The Hall Street Express serviced black domestics who rode out to the fashionable west end in the mornings and back down to the lower east side in the evenings.

"You know I can't stand being a chauffeur for a bunch of colored maids and cooks," he groused.

"Take it or leave it," Billy said, walking away in disgust.

Grady started to say something but thought better of it. He was still on probation, lucky even to have a job, especially during such hard times.

Snow had already begun to fall when Grady pulled out of the garage at 3:01. It fell steadily all afternoon, creating a frosted wonderland on the manicured lawns that lined West Hall. But by nightfall the winding, twisting, and bending street was a driver's nightmare.

The temperature plummeted, too, adding a new challenge to the mounting snow. "Hurry up! Hurry up! I can't wait all day," Grady snapped at the boarding passengers. "Get to the back of the bus," he hustled them on impatiently. "You people know the rules."

The regulars recognized Grady, but except for a few muffled groans they paid their fares and rode in sullen silence out to the east side loop.

"Auntie! Now, just why are you taking your own good time getting off this bus?" Grady grumbled at the last passenger.

The woman struggled down the wet, slippery steps. At the bottom she looked over her shoulder. Her dark face held no clue of any emotion. "Auntie? Did you really call me *Auntie?*" she said, laughing sarcastically. "Well, well, well! I never knew my brother had a white son." And she hurried away, chuckling.

Grady's face flushed with surprise and anger. He shouted out the door, "Don't get uppity with me! Y'all know *Auntie* is what we call all you old colored women." Furious, he slammed the door against the bitter cold. He shook his head in disgust. "It's a waste of time trying to be nice," he told himself.

But one look out the window made Grady refocus his attention to a more immediate problem. The weather had worsened. He checked his watch. It was a little past nine. Remarkably, he was still on schedule, but that didn't matter. He had decided to close down the route and take the bus in.

That's when his headlights picked up the figure of a woman running in the snow, without a hat, gloves, or boots. Although she'd pulled a shawl over the lightweight jacket and flimsy dress she was wearing, her clothing offered very little protection against the elements. As she pressed forward against the driving snow and wind, Grady saw that the woman was very young, no more than twenty. And she was clutching something close to her body. What was it? Then Grady saw the baby, a small bundle wrapped in a faded pink blanket.

"These people," Grady sighed, opening the door. The woman stumbled up the steps, escaping the wind that mercilessly ripped at her petite frame.

"Look here. I've closed down the route. I'm taking the bus in."

In big gulping sobs the woman laid her story before him. "I need help, please. My husband's gone to Memphis looking for work. Our baby's sick, real sick. She needs to get to the hospital. I know she'll die if I don't get help."

"Well, I got to go by the hospital on the way back to the garage. You can ride that far." Grady nodded for her to pay. The woman looked at the floor. "Well? Pay up and get on to the back of the bus so I can get out of here."

"I—I don't have the fare," she said, quickly adding, "but if you let me ride, I promise to bring it to you in the morning."

"Give an inch, y'all want a mile. You know the rules. No money, no ride!"

"Oh, please!" the young woman cried. "Feel her little head. It's so hot." She held out the baby to him. Grady recoiled.

Desperately the woman looked for something to bargain with. "Here," she said, taking off her wedding ring. "Take this. It's gold. But please don't make me get off this bus."

He opened the door. The winds howled savagely. "Please," the woman begged.

"Go on home, now. You young gals get hysterical over a little

fever. Nothing. It'll be fine in the morning.'' As he shut the door the last sounds he heard were the mother's sobs, the baby's wail, and the moaning wind.

Grady dismissed the incident until the next morning, when he read that it had been a record snowfall. His eyes were drawn to a small article about a colored woman and child found frozen to death on Hall Street. No one seemed to know where the woman was going or why. No one but Grady.

''That gal should have done like I told her and gone on home,'' he said, turning to the comics.

IT WAS EXACTLY one year later, on the anniversary of the record snowstorm, that Grady was assigned the Hall Street Express again. Just as before, a storm heaped several inches of snow onto the city in a matter of hours, making driving extremely hazardous.

By nightfall Grady decided to close the route. But just as he was making the turnaround at the east side loop, his headlight picked up a woman running in the snow—the same woman he'd seen the previous year. Death hadn't altered her desperation. Still holding on to the blanketed baby, the small-framed woman pathetically struggled to reach the bus.

Grady closed his eyes but couldn't keep them shut. She was still coming, but from where? The answer was too horrible to consider, so he chose to let his mind find a more reasonable explanation. From some dark corner of his childhood he heard his father's voice, slurred by alcohol, mocking him. *It ain't the same woman, dummy. You know how they all look alike!*

Grady remembered his father with bitterness and swore at the thought of him. This *was* the same woman, Grady argued with his father's memory, taking no comfort in being right. Grady watched the woman's movements breathlessly as she stepped out of the headlight beam and approached the door. She stood outside the door waiting . . . waiting.

The gray coldness of Fear slipped into the driver's seat. Grady sucked air into his lungs in big gulps, feeling out of control. Fear moved his foot to the gas pedal, careening the bus out into oncoming traffic. Headlights. A truck. Fear made Grady hit the brakes. The back of the bus went into a sliding spin, slamming into a tree. Grady's stomach crushed against the steering wheel, rupturing his liver and spleen. *You've really done it now, lunkhead.* As he drifted into the final darkness he heard a woman's sobs, a baby wailing—or was it just the wind?

TWENTY-FIVE YEARS later, Ray Hammond, a war hero with two years of college, became the first black driver Metro hired. A lot of things had happened during those two and a half decades to pave the way for Ray's new job. The military had integrated its forces during the Korean War. In 1954 the Supreme Court had ruled that segregated schools were unequal. And one by one, unfair laws were being challenged by civil rights groups all over the South. Ray had watched the Montgomery bus boycott with interest, especially the boycott's leader, Dr. Martin Luther King, Jr.

Ray soon found out that progress on the day-to-day level can be painfully slow. Ray was given the Hall Street Express.

"The white drivers call my route the Blackbird Express," Ray told his wife. "I'm the first driver to be given that route as a permanent assignment. The others wouldn't take it."

"What more did you expect?" his wife answered, tying his bow tie. "Just do your best so it'll be easier for the ones who come behind you."

In November, Ray worked the three-to-eleven shift. "Snow's predicted," the route manager barked one afternoon. "Close it down if it gets bad out there, Ray."

The last shift on the Hall Street Express.

Since he was a boy, Ray had heard the story of the haunting of that bus route. Every first snowfall passengers and drivers testified that they'd seen the ghost of Eula Mae Daniels clutching her baby as she ran through the snow.

"Good luck with Eula Mae tonight," one of the drivers said, snickering.

"I didn't know white folk believed in haints," Ray shot back.

But parked at the east side loop, staring into the swirling snow mixed with ice, Ray felt tingly, as if he were dangerously close to an electrical charge. He'd just made up his mind to close down the route and head back to the garage when he saw her. Every hair on his head stood on end.

He wished her away, but she kept coming. He tried to think, but his thoughts were jumbled and confused. He wanted to look away, but curiosity fixed his gaze on the advancing horror.

Just as the old porch stories had described her, Eula Mae Daniels was a small-framed woman frozen forever in youth. "So young," Ray whispered. "Could be my Carolyn in a few more years." He watched as the ghost came around to the doors. She was out there, waiting in the cold. Ray heard the baby crying. "There but for the grace of God goes one of mine," he said, compassion overruling his fear. "Nobody deserves to be left out in this weather. Ghost or not, she deserves better." And he swung open the doors.

The woman had form but no substance. Ray could see the snow

falling *through* her. He pushed fear aside. "Come on, honey, get out of the cold," Ray said, waving her on board.

Eula Mae stood stony still, looking up at Ray with dark, questioning eyes. The driver understood. He'd seen that look before, not from a dead woman but from plenty of his passengers. "It's okay. I'm for real. Ray Hammond, the first Negro to drive for Metro. Come on, now, get on," he coaxed her gently.

Eula Mae moved soundlessly up the steps. She held the infant to her body. Ray couldn't remember ever feeling so cold, not even the Christmas he'd spent in a Korean foxhole. He'd seen so much death, but never anything like this.

The ghost mother consoled her crying baby. Then with her head bowed she told her story in quick bursts of sorrow, just as she had twenty-five years earlier. "My husband is in Memphis looking for work. Our baby is sick. She'll die if I don't get help."

"First off," said Ray. "Hold your head up. You got no cause for shame."

"I don't have any money," she said. "But if you let me ride, I promise to bring it to you tomorrow. I promise."

Ray sighed deeply. "The rule book says no money, no ride. But the book doesn't say a word about a personal loan." He took a handful of change out of his pocket, fished around for a dime, and dropped it into the pay box. "You're all paid up. Now, go sit yourself down while I try to get this bus back to town."

Eula Mae started to the back of the bus.

"No you don't," Ray stopped her. "You don't have to sit in the back anymore. You can sit right up front."

The ghost woman moved to a seat closer, but still not too close up front. The baby fretted. The young mother comforted her as best she could.

They rode in silence for a while. Ray checked in the rearview mirror every now and then. She gave no reflection, but when he looked over his shoulder, she was there, all right. "Nobody will ever believe this," he mumbled. "*I* don't believe it.

"Things have gotten much better since you've been . . . away," he said, wishing immediately that he hadn't opened his mouth. Still he couldn't—or wouldn't—stop talking.

"I owe this job to a little woman just about your size named Mrs. Rosa Parks. Down in Montgomery, Alabama, one day, Mrs. Parks refused to give up a seat she'd paid for just because she was a colored woman."

Eula Mae sat motionless. There was no way of telling if she had heard or not. Ray kept talking. "Well, they arrested her. So the colored people decided to boycott the buses. Nobody rode for over a year. Walked everywhere, formed carpools, or just didn't go, rather than ride a bus. The man who led the boycott was named Reverend King. Smart man. We're sure to hear more about him in the future. . . . You still with me?" Ray looked around. Yes, she was there. The baby had quieted. It was much warmer on the bus now.

Slowly Ray inched along on the icy road, holding the bus steady, trying to keep the back wheels from racing out of control. "Where was I?" he continued. "Oh yeah, things changed after that Montgomery bus boycott. This job opened up. More changes are on the way. Get this: They got an Irish Catholic running for President. Now, what do you think of that?"

About that time Ray pulled the bus over at Seventeenth Street. The lights at Gale Hospital sent a welcome message to those in need on such a frosty night. "This is it."

Eula Mae raised her head. "You're a kind man," she said. "Thank you."

Ray opened the door. The night air gusted up the steps and nipped at his ankles. Soundlessly, Eula Mae stepped off the bus with her baby.

"Excuse me," Ray called politely. "About the bus fare. No need for you to make a special trip . . . back. Consider it a gift."

He thought he saw Eula Mae Daniels smile as she vanished into the swirling snow, never to be seen again.

The Conjure Brother

Until recently, most rural Southern towns had a resident conjure woman who sold her knowledge of the powers of roots and herbs for donations of food or clothing. Though some people laughed at the conjure woman's spells and potions, others swore by her ability to change luck or cure an ailment. Every now and then a conjure woman came along whose powers transcended those of the ordinary "root doctors." There was no limit to what she could do.

JOSIE WAS TIRED of being the only child in the Hudson family. Her friends JoBeth and Arthur Lee had lots of brothers and sisters between them. Josie wanted a brother.

"I'm the girl in the family," she reasoned. "Wouldn't it be nice to have a boy? Then I could be the sister and he could be the brother. What do you think?" Josie asked her mother.

Mama always had a ready answer. "I forgot to let the stork know we moved from Kennerly Street to Harrison Avenue last year," she said, taking plates down from the cabinet. Josie set the table. Mama smiled, then winked playfully. "So you see, he doesn't know where to bring a baby."

Josie knew better. Arthur Lee had told her and JoBeth how babies came into the world. "When your mother and father want a new baby, first your mama has to get fat," he'd said confidently. "She eats and eats until it looks like she's going to pop. But she doesn't. She goes to the hospital to lose the weight. Then they get to choose a baby. That's how it works."

Weeks passed and Mama stayed skinny. "She chews on celery," Josie told Arthur Lee and JoBeth at the sandbox. "I'll never get a brother."

"Well, my mama is big as a refrigerator," said Arthur Lee. "They say she'll be going to the hospital soon. If she brings home another baby boy, you can have him. I got four brothers, and that's enough!"

JoBeth added, "I saw in a magazine that you can adopt a baby from a faraway country for pennies a day."

No, Josie decided. "I want a brother that's the same as me."

"You don't always get what you want," Arthur Lee said. "Look at me."

"When my mother goes to the hospital, I'm going along to make sure they choose a brother."

Summer was passing quickly, and Mama was as thin as ever, snacking on carrot sticks. How could she get fat that way? Just when Josie was about to give up hope, she overheard Miz Annie and Miz Charlene talking about a conjure woman who had just moved to town.

"Reckon she could do something to change this streak of bad luck I been having?" Miz Annie asked.

Miz Charlene answered, "Yes, honey. I bet she could. She fixed me a salve that really helped my arthritis. And didn't charge me but a dozen eggs."

Their talk gave Josie an idea. Maybe the conjure woman could fix her up with a brother! That night Josie went to sleep thinking about what she and her new brother were going to do.

AT FIRST LIGHT Josie slipped out of her house. She gathered a basket of grapes to use as payment. Within the hour she was standing outside the conjure woman's house. A sign said: MADAM ZINNIA—SPELLS, POTIONS, AND SALVES—ALL WELCOME.

What did it look like inside? Josie wondered. Would there be bubbling pots and glowing bottles?

"Come in." A very attractive woman opened the door before Josie could knock. "I've been expecting you," she said, touching the side of Josie's face. "I see you've got a problem? Come, Josie, let Madam Zinnia help you."

Josie was impressed. Madam Zinnia knew her name and even knew she was coming. The girl stepped inside the house and looked around. There were no smoking skulls with cinder-hot eyes. No bats hanging from the ceiling, no bubbling jars of weird-looking stuff. In fact, the living room looked like a picture from a home magazine. It was a sunny room, cheerfully decorated with fresh-cut flowers and interesting whatnots.

Madam Zinnia matched her house in style and disposition. Dressed in a crisp yellow-and-white-checked shirtwaist and white heels, she looked like one of the saleswomen down at Hopperman's Dry Goods Store.

"Come have some fresh-squeezed orange juice and a just-from-the-oven biscuit," the woman said, ushering Josie into the kitchen.

This is all so *normal,* Josie thought.

Madam Zinnia poured two glasses of juice and took a seat at the kitchen table. Josie asked, "Would you please conjure me up a brother? I asked my mother to go to the hospital, but she's still skinny."

"Oh, chile, you can't go round ordering brothers like you do hot dogs at the ballpark."

"I know, but I've waited all summer."

"I see," Madam Zinnia said, giving an understanding nod. "A brother may not be what you really want. I know, because Madam has one. Oh, what a rascal," she said, fanning her face with her pocket handkerchief. "Let Madam conjure you up a fine pet instead."

"My brother will be different."

"Well, a brother you shall have." And closing her eyes tightly, Madam Zinnia said some words Josie didn't know. Then she gave the girl a formula to conjure a brother. "You must do just as I say. Don't change a thing. Find a peach tree twig. Don't strip the leaves. Slide it under your bed from the left side. Then at exactly one minute after midnight, climb into bed from the right side and go to sleep saying whatever name you want to give your brother. Come morning, you'll have a beautiful baby brother."

Josie hurried home and followed the conjure instructions precisely—well, almost. As hard as she tried, she couldn't stay awake until midnight. So she did the conjure spell at ten o'clock instead, and she fell asleep calling her brother's name. "Adam . . . Adam . . . Adam!"

THE NEXT MORNING Josie woke to the smell of country ham

and eggs, grits, and biscuits. She rushed into the kitchen. The table was set for four.

"Whose plate is that?" Josie asked, pointing to a place opposite her side of the table.

"Yours," Mama answered, looking at the girl askance.

Josie was surprised, because she'd sat on the right side as long as she'd sat in a chair. "Then whose plate is that?"

"Don't start something with your brother this morning," Mama said, stirring the pot vigorously. "You know very well that's Adam's place."

"My *brother* Adam?" Josie shouted. "It worked, Mama. I conjured up a brother for myself. Isn't it wonderful? Where is he?"

Mama laughed. "You read too many of those fantasy books, Josie."

But the girl didn't hear. She had bounded out the back door. Mama shrugged and went back to cooking.

Suddenly Josie stopped in her tracks. Something wasn't quite right. Adam was supposed to be a baby. But he was old enough to have a place at the table. Oh, well, she thought. A brother is a brother.

Josie looked behind the garage. "Adam," she called. "Oh, Adam."

All at once someone grabbed her from behind. "You thought you'd catch me off guard. But I gotcha."

Josie tried to turn so she could see her brother, but he held on fast. "Is that you, Adam?" she yelled. "Adam?"

"I won't let you go unless you play In My Power."

"Okay," Josie said, letting him hook his baby finger in hers. "I'm in your power."

Adam let her go immediately. "Okay, who are you? You aren't

Josie Hudson. My real sister wouldn't play In My Power without a big fight."

Josie smiled and looked at Adam with wide wondering eyes. He was a shorter version of Daddy, minus a mustache. And though he was frowning at her, the light in his eyes sparkled like sunlight on Mama's chandelier. "But you're my *real* brother," she said. "And we're going to have fun together. I'd love to play In My Power with you, honest. We'll play whatever you want to play."

Adam backed away humming the *Twilight Zone* theme music. "Earth to Josie. Earth to Josie. Tune in, girl."

Mama called for breakfast, and Adam hurried away. Josie skipped behind, making plans for all the wonderful things she was going to do with her conjure brother.

BY THE END of the week Josie's joy had turned sour. Nobody seemed to notice that Adam was a conjured brother. It was like he had *always been.* And what made it worse, Adam was the oldest.

Mama and Daddy looked at Adam as if he were something very, very special. He got to ride up front and sit next to Daddy in church. Adam got to cross the pike all by himself and stay up half an hour later at night. How come?

"'Cause I was here first," he teased. Then, snatching the last cookie from the cookie jar, he ran out the door.

"But I didn't ask for an older brother," she complained to Madam Zinnia. "I thought my brother was supposed to be a little baby. What happened?"

The conjure woman stopped weeding her garden, stood, and took off her sunbonnet. "Ahhh, flowers take time and lots of care to grow so pretty," she said, wiping her brow. "Okay, now what's this about the conjure not working? Did you do exactly as I told you?"

Josie looked down at her feet. "Not quite. I couldn't stay awake until midnight, so I did it all at ten o'clock."

Madam Zinnia shook her head. "Why do people mess with my stuff? That's what happened," she said, snipping roses. "If you had done the conjure at one minute past midnight, the beginning of a new day, you would have gotten a new life, a baby. But you went to sleep at ten, so you got a ten-year-old brother. Sorry, but Madam cannot guarantee a conjure unless it is done properly. I'm afraid you have to live with your big brother."

Josie helped Madam Zinnia plant a beautiful yellow rosebush. "Yellow roses are my favorite," the woman said later, pouring Josie a glass of lemonade. "It takes patience to grow them, lots and lots of patience."

ALL THE NEXT WEEK Josie tried to make the best of a bad situation. No matter what Adam did, Josie went along with it. But the harder she tried, the worse Adam got. "What's wrong with you, silly girl?" he shouted angrily. "You're not acting right. You're so—so stupid!"

"I try to get along with him," Josie told JoBeth at the swings.

"Stop trying so hard," said JoBeth. "Fight back."

So that's what Josie did. That same evening Adam wanted to watch an old movie, but she'd waited all day for her favorite comedy show. She turned the channel, and he pushed her out of the way and flipped it back. Josie fired off a punch to Adam's chin. He hit her back—hard.

"I hate you," she said, wiping away angry tears. "I wish it was just me again."

"Just you," Adam snapped back. "It was great around here until we found you on the railroad tracks and brought you home."

"That's not true!" Josie cried harder. Adam smiled. Daddy broke up the fight and sent them both to bed early with no television. Josie cried herself to sleep.

Arthur Lee and JoBeth came by first thing the next morning. "We haven't gone over to the pike to watch the big trucks go by in weeks."

"Want to go with us?"

Josie ran to get her bicycle out of the garage. It wasn't there. "Mama, where's my bicycle?"

Mama sighed. "Josie, what are you talking about?" she asked impatiently. "You're the one who made the decision. Adam got the bicycle and you got the chemistry set and the doll dishes."

Josie was shattered. Last Christmas she'd gotten it all—the bicycle, the chemistry set, and the doll dishes.

She rode double on Arthur Lee's bike, feeling awful. The three friends sat on the retaining wall and watched the big wheelers roll past, moving at high speeds. Sometimes the truckers tooted their horns and waved. Usually Josie liked to imitate the sound the trucks made as they passed—"Whoosh! Whoosh!" But she didn't feel like having fun this morning.

"Are big brothers always so awful?" Josie asked.

"Not always," Arthur Lee answered.

"I can't beat Adam up. What should I do?"

"Get even. That's what I do," said JoBeth.

"Good idea," Josie replied.

Josie put her plan into motion.

Adam had a crush on Lillie, JoBeth's big sister. Josie asked Adam to go with her and JoBeth to the movies. Of course he said no. "JoBeth's big sister is taking her." Adam took the bait—hook, line, and sinker. He agreed to go before he knew it was a horror movie, *Return of the Vampire Mummy.* Adam hated horror movies, but he wouldn't dare admit it. Everything was working perfectly.

At last Saturday came. JoBeth, Lillie, Josie, and Adam met in front of the Ritz. Josie could hardly keep a straight face. During the movie, Josie saw Adam close his eyes when the vampire mummy pushed open the tomb or bit somebody on the neck. And at the end, when the monster shriveled away to dust, Adam slunk down in his seat. Josie knew he was scared to death. Wonderful!

All the kids who lived on Harrison walked home together after the show. It wasn't dark yet, but the sun had set and lengthy shadows flickered in the last golden light. Josie knew Adam was thinking about vampires that rose at sunset.

As they approached a stretch of vacant property strewn with weeds and trash, Adam moved up to walk with Lillie. Suddenly a caped figure leaped out of nowhere. In the waning light they saw the hideously deformed creature with horrible vampire teeth confronting them.

All eyes were on Adam. The creature reached out to him. He gasped, his face turned green, and he ran away screaming in terror. Arthur Lee took off his Halloween mask and they all laughed. "He's not so tough and mean now. That'll teach him," said Josie.

But she didn't get the last laugh after all. Adam had gotten home and told his side of the story first. Mama was plenty mad. "What a mean thing to do, Josie Marie Hudson."

"I can't help it if Adam is a scaredy-cat."

"There's nothing wrong with being frightened, but there *is* something wrong with being mean. Embarrassing your brother in front of his friends was unkind and you owe him an apology."

"I won't apologize," Josie said defiantly.

"Don't sass me, girl. What's wrong with you, anyway? For the past few weeks the two of you have been at each other's throats. I've had enough and I want it to stop!"

"I do too," Josie sobbed, and hurried to her room.

MORNING CAME. Josie picked a basket of ripe tomatoes from Mama's garden and went to see Madam Zinnia. "Adam is a conjure brother and I don't want him anymore. Will you give me a spell to make him go away?" she begged, presenting Madam Zinnia with the tomatoes.

"What did that wretched boy do?" Madam Zinnia asked.

"He teases me all the time."

"I have just the thing for a teaser. Madam will put him in a cage and call forth nasty little gremlins to poke at him all day with sticks." And with a wink she raised her hand. "That will fix him good."

"Stop!" the girl shouted. "He's not that bad. He's just bossy."

"Bossy big brothers! I know about that. Yes, Madam will make him the servant of a terrible beast who lives between the pages of a book." And she raised her hand as if to send him there.

"No," Josie stopped her. "Don't do that. He's not *that* bossy. He just wants his way all the time."

"Yes. I'll turn him into a big rock sitting in the middle of nowhere. Rocks never get their way about anything."

Josie thought about Adam being a rock. She shook her head. "No, he's not really so bad. We did have some fun times together. And sometimes I did things to him that weren't so nice either. Oh, I'm all confused."

"I see," said Madam Zinnia, cutting a lovely yellow rose. "Think about it, little one," she said, putting the bloom in the girl's hair, "then tell me, what have you learned from all this?"

"Being the youngest is hard!"

"What a good lesson to learn. I hope you will remember that when you are a big sister . . . one day soon."

"Really? Oh, wow! Wait until I tell Adam."

"But remember," the woman called, "you must be patient."

A SUNBEAM tickled Josie awake. Mama called her to breakfast, but the kitchen table was only set for three. There was no sign of Adam. He was gone—or had he ever been?

Mama was talking on the telephone. When she hung up, she was smiling. She ran to hug Daddy. "That was the doctor's office. Something wonderful is going to happen," she said. "We're going to have a new baby come January. I hope it will be the brother you've been wanting."

Josie clapped her hands and turned round and round, laughing. "I don't care if it's a boy anymore. Oh, and I'm going to be the best *big sister* in the whole wide world."

"I bet you will," Mama said, laughing too.

Josie was delighted that she was finally getting her wish, but deep down inside she wondered about Adam. Had it all been just a dream? Hopping onto her bicycle, she rode as fast as she could to Madam Zinnia's house.

It was empty and there was a FOR RENT sign in the yard. "Where did Madam Zinnia go?" Josie asked the mailman, who happened to be passing by.

"Madam who? I deliver to a Madam Zonobia, a palm reader over on Lee Avenue. But nobody's lived in this house all summer."

Josie looked at the well-kept flower garden and the lovely yellow rosebush by the side of the house and smiled.

Boo Mama

The year 1968 was full of conflict and contradictions, a tumultuous time of highs and lows. Although blacks and whites were dying together in Vietnam, a distant country in Southeast Asia, at home the races were divided over basic human rights. Nobel Peace Prize winner Martin Luther King, Jr., was killed in Memphis, Tennessee. His death was followed by days of rioting. Two months later, Robert F. Kennedy, brother of assassinated president John F. Kennedy, was himself assassinated after winning the California Democratic primary.

When the day-to-day grind got to be a bit too much for some, a few people chose to "drop out." At the time there was a saying: "Stop the world, I want to get off." But since the world could not be stopped, many people just walked away.

FROM THE AGE OF sixteen Leddy had been an activist, committed to nonviolent action against racism and discrimination. While in college, she'd participated in sit-ins, freedom rides, voter registration campaigns, and peace protests. Later, working in Memphis, Leddy had met and married Lieutenant Joe Morrison, U.S. Marine Corps. Two months before their son Nealy was born, Joe had been shipped out to Vietnam. He was killed six months later.

With her husband's funeral still fresh in her memory, Leddy heard the news that Martin Luther King, Jr., had been killed in Memphis at the Lorraine Motel. Although violence was contrary to everything Dr. King had stood for, Leddy longed for a physical outlet for her rage. "What is this world coming to?" she whispered.

On the morning of June 7, 1968, Leddy addressed a small group who'd gathered outside the storefront office of the Center for Progress Through Peace, where she worked. "Yes, it's true. It's true. Robert Kennedy is dead. Martin was for peace and he was killed. Malcolm X said fight back and he was killed. Robert Kennedy said stop this senseless war, and now he's dead!" Leddy was screaming at this point. "Anybody who stands up for right gets shot in this country! Robert Kennedy is dead! Love, peace, equality, justice, and freedom have died, too!"

Someone snatched the mike and pulled her inside the building.

"Hey, cool it." It was Germaine, director of the C.P.T.P. and a veteran civil rights activist. "Don't start a riot," he said firmly, though his eyes were gentle and kind.

Since Joe's death, Germaine and his wife, Sylvia, had been like parents to Leddy, taking mother and son in, giving Leddy a job.

Leddy wouldn't deliberately hurt Germaine or the Center. But she felt herself spinning out of control. She trembled with emotion. "That's it! I'm sick and tired of cooling it! I'm burning up with *cool!*" Leddy paced back and forth as she talked. "I was *cool* when a woman put a loaded shotgun to my head just because I was sitting at an all-white lunch counter. I stayed *cool* when firemen turned hoses on me for peacefully protesting the murder of innocent children in a church bombing. I was *cool* when they murdered Martin Luther King. And I was *supercool* when they told me that little Nealy would never see his father, because Joe had been killed in a place most of us can't pronounce. Don't talk to me about being *cool,* Germaine! What has being *cool* done for me? Nothing!"

"Okay, okay," Germaine said gently. "Just calm down, now."

Leddy covered her face with her hands and wept. "I'm so tired," she sobbed. Germaine handed her a tissue, and she wiped her eyes. "For all our efforts, what has changed, Germaine? Are people living in better housing? Are people getting good health care? Is it really better now than it was ten, twenty years ago? I wanted so much more for my son."

Germaine sighed. "So did I. We all did."

GERMAINE AND SYLVIA and all her friends at the Center tried to talk Leddy into staying, but she'd made up her mind. She was going to get out of Memphis.

"I realize now," she said, stepping on board the bus, "that there's no way for me to change the world, but I do have something to say about the piece of earth where I live. We're going where I hope it will be better."

"When you get settled, write us," Germaine said with fatherly concern. "Take care."

Orchard City, situated in the mountains of eastern Tennessee, seemed an ideal spot to make a fresh start. Using some of her military survivor's benefits, Leddy bought the old Lippincott place up on Orchard Mountain. What the new home lacked in modern conveniences, comfort, and style, it made up for in beauty and peace.

The rural community received the outsider coolly at first, thinking she might be the advance guard of a hippie invasion. Leddy didn't care. Nealy seemed to thrive in the new environment, and Leddy took joy in watching him romp and play freely in the solitude of their mountain home.

But that peace was shattered when Nealy disappeared into the woods out behind the house one spring morning. Leddy charged into Sheriff Pete Martin's office, on the verge of collapse.

"My baby," she cried, gasping for breath. "I—I was hanging out wash. Nealy was beside me, but when I turned around, he was gone. He must have wandered into the woods. I looked and looked. Please come. I need help."

"Don't get yourself all in a stew," the sheriff said calmly. "Nealy ain't the first youngun who's gone and got hisself lost in the woods. Usually we find 'em perched on a ledge too scared to move." His words were meant to be kind, but Leddy was unconvinced.

Sheriff Martin put together a search party and they combed Orchard Mountain from bottom to top and back down again. Nothing. Not a clue.

When they hadn't found Nealy by nightfall, an uneasiness settled over the searchers.

"A two-year-old ain't got much chance up here alone," Leddy overheard one of the men say. She knew it was true. Orchard Mountain challenged the best hikers and hunters, and some of them had to be brought out by helicopter.

Finally Jay Wilson's hounds tracked the boy's trail to a ledge, where they found his brown teddy bear.

"It's Nealy's favorite toy," Leddy told the sheriff. Her lip quivered, but she refused to cry. "He—he called it Boo!"

Sheriff Martin couldn't hide the concern on his face. Leddy saw it and responded. "If he fell from that ledge," she argued, "then where is his body?"

"Wild animals . . ."

The story preempted the Vietnam War news for three days running. A Boy Scout troop came from Knoxville to join in the search, and a motorcycle club also helped. Germaine and Sylvia even came to aid their friend but by the end of the week the media had withdrawn, and the volunteers had, one by one, given up hope and gone home. "I'd keep a-looking," Sheriff Martin told Leddy, "but without leads, I don't know where to start."

Germaine and Sylvia were the last to leave. When Leddy was alone, she let herself cry. "I'll never stop looking for you, baby," she sobbed. Then she dried her eyes and pulled herself tall. "I know you're not dead. A mother knows such things."

Leddy refused to leave her mountain home more than an hour at a time, hoping Nealy might come back. Day after day she went to the woods and called the boy's name over and over.

"Ain't a bit natural," the women said when they heard her pitiful cries. "Leddy needs to forget about that baby. He's dead for sure, and holding on to hope when there ain't no hope just ain't natural."

Leddy knew what they were saying, but she stubbornly refused to despair. "My baby will be back," she said. "I know it."

LEDDY'S FAITH paid off. One year, two months, three days, and four hours after his disappearance, Nealy was found on the steps of the Mount Olive African Methodist Episcopal Church, naked as a jay and smelling like he'd tangled with a family of skunks. Except for a few scratches and a lot of chigger bites, he seemed none the worse.

Reverend Clyde Anderson sent somebody to get Leddy. Meanwhile, he declared Nealy's return a miracle and Mother Jacobs sang "Amazing Grace." There hadn't been that kind of spirit in the AME Church since Old Abe, the town drunk, put down the bottle and joined church. The whole congregation was moved to tears when Leddy laid eyes on her son for the first time in more than a year.

The boy's return raised a lot of questions, and Sheriff Martin decided to reopen the case to get answers. Where had Nealy been? Who with? Why was he taken? Why did they bring him back? Or did he find his way back alone?

The investigation began with Nealy being given complete physical and psychological examinations at the university hospital in Knoxville. When asked about his experiences, the boy offered no help. He made lots of sounds, but the team of pediatricians who examined him thought it was just baby talk.

Sheriff Martin joined Leddy in the conference room.

"Except for your son's delayed communication skills," Dr. Jamison, the chief doctor, explained to Leddy, "little Nealy is in remarkable shape." The doctor groped for words. "But he shouldn't be. Your son's body shows signs of extreme trauma."

Pointing to the x-rays, the doctor said, "There have been severe injuries to his spine, lungs, liver, and spleen. Such injuries should have killed him. But through some miraculous healing process this child got well. I've never seen anything like it."

Another doctor immediately began his report. "I've examined Nealy's lab work, and frankly I don't know what's going on. His blood cells look healthy, but they are slightly altered—a mutation of some kind that we've never seen before. We'd have to do many more tests to determine that."

Next, the child psychologist introduced herself and gave her report. "Mrs. Morrison, contrary to what we suspected when we saw the x-rays, Nealy has no brain damage, either. He's alert, responsive, interacts well with others. Your child is a healthy, active three-year-old—and very, very bright. However, his verbal skills confuse me. I don't agree with my colleagues that it's just jibberish. I'd like to do more tests, too."

Leddy looked at Nealy playing on the floor. He seemed curious about everything, pointing first to one thing, then another, and jibber-jabbering nonstop. "I must admit your reports are disturbing. But tell me this. Is my son okay?"

"We don't have a lot of answers," Dr. Jamison said. "But one thing is for sure. Somebody has taken very good care of this child. He's in excellent physical condition."

"Who?" Sheriff Martin interrupted. "That's what I want to know. Who took this child, and why? I don't believe in the little green men in the spaceship," he said.

Leddy raised her hand for them to stop. "I don't care about who, why, or where. Nealy is back with me, and that's all that matters."

The doctors pleaded with Leddy to let them study the boy longer, but Leddy wouldn't allow it. "Don't you think my child has been through enough? Maybe later I'll let you do more tests, but not now."

And she retreated to the mountain and began piecing their lives back together.

IT DIDN'T take long for Leddy to start noticing things about Nealy—curious things that troubled her. He refused meat and sweets, choosing a fresh apple over a piece of Leddy's homemade apple pie every time.

But stranger still was the rate of Nealy's hair growth. Even accounting for longer styles, his hair needed to be trimmed almost every day. Leddy noticed something else. Nealy no longer sucked his thumb and he was potty-trained.

"Who helped you break those habits but didn't teach you to talk?" she wondered.

The boy was full of sounds, but they made no sense. As he tried to understand or make himself understood, Nealy got confused and cried. Sometimes the child wept softly, for no reason Leddy could figure out, or he'd stand in the backyard looking toward the woods, making guttural noises.

The doctors had told Leddy that Nealy had delayed language skills. They suggested she talk to him a lot and read to him regularly. But reading time was the most frustrating part of the day for both mother and child. Though Nealy seemed eager, he lost interest as soon as Leddy began.

"Oh, Nealy," she said, on the verge of tears. "I'm trying so hard. Please be patient with me."

"Toi ben tu," Nealy said, snuggling against her. *"Toi ben tu,"* he repeated.

Leddy didn't know what the boy meant, but she smiled and kissed him. "I love you, little boy. And don't you ever forget it."

Then one day Leddy stumbled on to something. "Let's have a glass of orange juice," she said, showing Nealy the carton.

Nealy shook his head. *"Saawa,"* he said, pointing to a pitcher of water. *"Saawa."*

After nervously pouring a glass of water, Leddy handed it to her son. *"Saawa."* She repeated the word he'd used.

Nealy took it, smiling proudly because he'd finally made himself understood. After gulping down the water, he bounded off, chattering and squealing playfully.

Leddy followed behind him, desperate to know more. "Read," she said, holding up a book.

"Froce," he said, taking it and climbing up onto his mother's lap. Opening the book, Leddy pointed to the colorful pictures. "Bird," she said.

Nealy covered his mother's mouth with his hand and shook his head. *"Naga,"* he said. *"Naga."*

The next page. "Tree."

"Pota."

Leddy turned the page to a large brown bear. Nealy touched the picture with remembering fingers. "Boo Mama." He clapped his hands and giggled. Then, trying to lift the image off the page, he shouted, "Boo Mama!" He kissed the picture. *"Toi ben tu,* Boo Mama!"

Leddy's heart leaped with joy. "You remember," she said, putting Nealy down and rushing to the hall closet. Rummaging through a box, she found the tattered brown bear Nealy had affectionately called Boo.

She offered it to Nealy, but he pushed it away. "No. Boo Mama," he said, pointing out the window and growing more fretful.

"This is Boo. Don't you recognize your friend Boo?"

No matter how hard Leddy tried, Nealy wouldn't be comforted. Looking out the window, he called again and again, "Boo Mama. Boo Mama. Boo Mama."

That night Nealy cried himself to sleep. And so did Leddy.

AT FIRST LIGHT, Leddy and Nealy caught the bus to Knoxville. The first place she stopped was the language lab at the university. She gave them Nealy's words and asked that they translate them and identify what language they were from. They told her it would take a few days to research, but if she'd leave a self-addressed, stamped envelope, they promised to forward their findings.

Then she went to the library and found several books about child development. Nealy paged through a picture book while Leddy read: "Children often make up their own words for things. They create imaginary playmates and creatures with whom they can share a secret world."

On the way to the bus station she and Nealy stopped to get ice cream. He seemed to enjoy the treat and laughed when it touched his nose.

"Thank . . . you . . . Mama," he said haltingly. "Thank you."

"Oh, Nealy!" Leddy shouted for joy. "You said words! And you called me *mama!*"

"Toi ben tu, Mama," he said.

Leddy was more convinced than ever that Nealy's strange talking was only a developmental phase. He was going to be fine—just fine.

IT HAD BEEN a wonderful day, until Leddy undressed Nealy for bed. A strip of hair had grown down the middle of his back. Leddy touched it with shaking hands. Overcome by guilt, Leddy reprimanded herself. "Maybe you should have let the doctors do more tests." But as she held Nealy close in her arms, she felt comforted.

Finally Nealy went to sleep. Exhausted, Leddy fell across her bed and fell asleep, too. She was awakened by a mournful wail that rose from the woods, filling the night with horror. Then came a metallic odor—a foul mixture of sulfur and coal—that she recognized as the smell that had been on Nealy when he came back.

Leddy rushed to the boy's room. He wasn't in his bed, under it, or in the closet.

She heard footsteps outside the house and looked up in time to see a large shadow move across the window. Was it a bear? Any minute she expected a wild animal to crash through the door. Leddy dropped to her hands and knees so as not to be seen, then crawled down the hallway. "Nealy!" she whispered. "Where are you?"

"Mama!" he said, running to her from the bathroom. "Mama," he said, taking her hand and leading her to the kitchen. He wanted her to open the back door.

"No," Leddy said, pulling him away. "Come here." There was someone—something—at the back door. She could hear it breathing. Leddy held on to the boy tightly, but he struggled to free himself. "Boo Mama!"

Confused and terrified, Leddy yelled to the intruder, "Leave us alone. Please go away!"

It was hard to tell how long she sat on the floor holding Nealy, too afraid to move. At last, when she thought it was safe, Leddy stood up and peered out the window, searching the moonlit backyard for signs of life.

"Mama," Nealy said, reaching up. Leddy lifted him to the kitchen counter. He looked out the window and waved. "Boo Mama," he said, pointing to the woods. A moonbeam fell across the boy's face and Leddy saw, to her horror, that his eyes were flame red.

MORNING ARRIVED on a spectacular note. Spring was inching its way up Orchard Mountain, but Leddy paid no mind to the flowering dogwoods that laced the woods. She ventured into the trees for another reason.

With a shotgun hoisted over her shoulder and Nealy in tow, she waited, not knowing what to expect.

Right away she felt watched. Suddenly the normal hum of the woods had stopped. The absolute silence was unsettling. "Now is the hour. Stay cool," she said, steeling her nerve and proceeding with the plan.

Circling the area, Leddy returned to the clearing out behind the house. "Stay here in the backyard, Nealy," she ordered. "I'm going into the house to get us some water."

No sooner was she inside the door than the powerful odor came. Nealy recognized it and started toward the woods. "Boo Mama," he called, his arms outstretched.

By using an old hunters' trick, Leddy had doubled back through the house and reentered the woods from downwind. She hid in a clump of bushes that gave her a clear view of Nealy. He stood in a clearing, calling, "Boo Mama." With the shotgun leveled and steady, she saw something incredible.

A hairy creature, big like a bear but with human features, emerged from a clump of bushes opposite Leddy. Without a single measure of fear or repulsion, Nealy rushed toward the creature, jabbering in his unknown tongue.

Gently the creature bent to scoop the child in its enormous arms, enveloping him with a big hug. "Boo Mama!" Nealy squealed happily.

Leddy watched the bizarre reunion with a mixture of fear and surprise. She was bewildered by the obvious trust and affection Nealy had for the creature. None of it made sense. Stepping from the safety of her hiding place, she aimed the shotgun at the creature's head. "Put my baby down, or I'll blow you to kingdom come."

The creature pivoted and lowered Nealy to the ground. The boy clung to its legs.

"Come to me, Nealy," Leddy ordered in her no-nonsense voice, holding out her arm.

Nealy was confused and looked to the creature for permission.

It nodded. "Mama." The boy walked toward Leddy, looking back to make sure his friend was still there.

"Who? What are you?" Leddy asked. "What have you done to my child?"

The creature remained motionless, gazing at the gun with wondering red eyes.

Leddy studied the creature cautiously. "You're not a bear or an ape," she reasoned.

No response. "Look," Leddy said, "if you can understand me, please say something . . . do something to show me you don't want to hurt Nealy and me."

Still no response. "Look at my son's eyes!" she screamed. "Look at his back! He's changing into—what?" Hot tears stung Leddy's face. She pushed Nealy behind her. "Please tell me what's going on. What have you done to him? Try to understand, Nealy is all I have in the world."

The creature sighed. "I know." The voice was thick and raspy but clearly female. Speaking slowly, she said, "I brought him back to you."

Nealy slipped from around his mother and rushed toward the creature. "Boo Mama!"

"So you're the one he calls Boo Mama—it makes sense," Leddy whispered, remembering Nealy's teddy bear. There was a gentleness about the creature that eased Leddy's fear. Feeling less threatened, she lowered the gun.

The creature explained, "You call us Sasquatch—Big Foot. We are the Gen. We are human, but different. Sun is not good for us. We live deep inside the mountain. There are others like us—everywhere."

"Why did you take Nealy?"

"I found him hurt. He fell from a ledge." Leddy gasped. "He was mostly dead," the creature continued. "He needed blood or he would die. So we transfused him with our blood. We didn't know what would happen. But Nealy lived."

Leddy looked at Nealy's red eyes and fought back tears. His hair had grown overnight to shoulder length. Patches of hair were growing on the backs of his hands. "Is he changing into one of you?"

"Yes. We should have kept the boy. But you cried and cried. I heard and brought him back."

"How long will it take before he looks like—like you?"

"We don't know."

Leddy felt helpless. She kicked at the dirt with the toe of her shoe, then slumped on a nearby rock ledge. She wanted to hate the creature, but in spite of herself she couldn't. After all, it had saved Nealy's life.

"What is your name? I know you only as Boo Mama," Leddy said.

"I am Noss," the creature said, sitting beside Leddy. Nealy played contentedly between the two of them, and as much as her limited English would allow, Noss talked about her civilization. Her people had conquered disease, overcome hatred and greed, and harnessed resources within the earth to prolong life. Noss was one hundred seventy years old, but considered middle-aged.

Leddy sighed. "A lot of people have been locked up, beaten, and even killed for daring to dream of such a world," she said, remembering.

Darkness always came to the woods faster. Noss sniffed the air, then ended the conversation by standing. Leddy grew uncomfortable. She hopped to her feet, too. "I'd better be going now," she said, taking Nealy's hand.

Noss blocked her way. "The boy must come with me. He can no longer live in your world. He will die."

Leddy felt her knees buckle. "No," she said, grasping at straws. "There must be some other way."

"No," Noss said, calling Nealy in her language.

"No!" Leddy said, raising the shotgun. "Come to me, baby."

The child looked from one to the other. "Mama. Boo Mama."

Noss spoke to the boy in her language.

The boy answered, "*Toi ben tu,* Boo Mama. *Toi ben tu,* Mama."

Noss turned to Leddy, and in a single movement she took the shotgun and twisted it into a heap of metal. "He says he loves us both. What if you and Nealy both come with me?"

"You want *me* to come too?"

"It is your choice."

Leddy looked at Nealy. His red eyes sparkled beneath bushy eyebrows. "*Toi ben tu,* Mama," he said, smiling.

"*Toi ben tu,* Nealy," Leddy answered. "More than anything in *this* world."

FOR A WHILE folks in Orchard City talked about Nealy and Leddy's disappearance from the mountain. Finally they decided that even though they left all their belongings, there was no sign of foul play. Perhaps Leddy and the boy had relocated somewhere else.

That explanation satisfied everybody except Leddy's old friends and Sheriff Martin. Every now and then Germaine and Sylvia would come up to Orchard Mountain. They'd go to Leddy's place and look around, hoping to find something that might explain her disappearance. Sheriff Martin helped, despite the fact that his inventory of clues was scanty. In the clearing he'd found a twisted shotgun and a series of footprints that led nowhere. In the house he'd found a letter from the university stating that the words Leddy wanted looked up—*saawa, froce, naga, porta*—weren't part of any known language.

Standing on the ledge where Nealy's teddy bear had turned up, they discussed a scrap of paper, the clue they felt was the key to solving the case. Why, they wondered, had Leddy written BOO MAMA and underscored it several times?

The Gingi

There is a universal folk theme that repeatedly warns: Evil needs an invitation. One of the many stories based on this idea comes from the Yoruba people of Nigeria, West Africa, who believe an evil spirit can't enter a house without first being welcomed. To trick an unsuspecting victim into freely letting it enter, the malevolent force uses clever and beguiling disguises. So a charm or an amulet was always used by the Yoruba as protection against evil. Today most people reject the mystical beliefs of their ancestors, but they keep a talisman around—like a rabbit's foot, a four-leaf clover, or a gingi—just in case.

LAURA PAUSED to look in the window of the Mother Africa Shop. She smiled when she saw the small ebony figure of a squatting woman with her arms folded around her knees. It was a pose her four-year-old daughter Lizzie took whenever she discovered something fascinating in the grass and wanted to observe it more closely.

Laura decided to go inside. But as she approached the door she gasped and stepped back. Glaring at her from the window was a hideous toothless hag with burning silver-hot eyes.

But once in the shop Laura saw no one. Where'd that thing come from? she wondered. She blamed stress—with a big *S*—the culprit of the nineties. Moving to a new city and a new job, all in the past eight months, had finally taken its toll.

Picking up the ebony sculpture she'd admired from the window, Laura said, "I have a perfect place for you." The figurine felt smooth and warm to the touch. "Yes," Laura whispered. "I will take you home with me."

A Ghanaian woman came to the front of the store, dressed in Western clothing except for an Asante head wrap. She was well over six feet, yet to Laura her movements seemed as graceful and fluid as a dancer's. "I am Mrs. Aswadi," the woman said cordially. "How may I help you?"

"How much is this piece?" Laura asked.

Mrs. Aswadi looked confused, almost startled. "I—I don't know. In fact, I've never seen it before. Where'd you find it?"

Laura pointed to the window display.

"That's strange," the woman said. "This is definitely not an Asante design. And all my pieces are Asante." She studied the sculpture more carefully. "It looks Yoruban to me."

"I'd still like to buy it."

Worry lines creased Mrs. Aswadi's forehead as she turned the figure over and over in her hand. Her eyes fluttered, and she whispered something in a language Laura didn't recognize. Then shifting to English, Mrs. Aswadi said, "I feel this is a wicked thing—very old and very powerful." She paused. "Among the Yoruba there are terrible spirits known as the Dabobo. The Dabobo disguise themselves and wait to be taken into a home—their evil nature is awakened by this invitation."

Laura laughed. "I don't believe in such things. This is just a piece of wood."

"No," Mrs. Aswadi insisted. "That is what the spirit wants you to think. Once you willingly take it into your home, you unlock its rage. You and your family could be in grave danger."

"Oh, please," Laura protested. "You can't expect me to believe something so outrageous. Are you going to sell the piece or not?"

Mrs. Aswadi stiffened. "You African Americans have forgotten so much of Africa." She sighed, then pulled herself tall. "Fifty dollars."

The price was too high and they both knew it. Laura decided it was time to leave. But when she touched the figure again, tracing its shape with her fingers, she realized she had to have it. Resigning herself, she paid twenty dollars more than it was worth.

The transaction was completed in silence. Not feeling the least bit triumphant, Laura started toward the door. Mrs. Aswadi rushed from behind the counter. "Wait," she called, all of her cool reserve melting away. With genuine concern in her eyes, she thrust a small object into Laura's free hand. "This is a gift. I always give a gift to customers who buy fifty dollars' worth of merchandise or more," she said. "Keep it with you."

LAURA WOKE with a start, frightening August, the family's big gray tomcat, who'd been napping at the foot of her bed.

"Who's there?" she called out, feeling a presence. The bedroom was dark even though it was the middle of the afternoon. She threw back the heavy drapes and August hopped to the window sill, playfully batting at a moving shadow.

"What a strange day," Laura mumbled, noticing she'd fallen asleep in her clothes, something she never did. She cut on the water in the bathroom sink and started to wash her face when suddenly she drew back, gasping. Someone was standing behind her. She whirled around, but the figure had disappeared. "Is anyone there?" Laura rushed out of the bathroom, expecting to find an intruder.

As she went back into the bathroom she heard August meow. "This whole afternoon has been surreal," she said to her own image, "especially Mrs. Aswadi and the Mother Africa Shop. No wonder I'm seeing stuff." Then casually reaching inside her jacket pocket, she discovered a little straw and cloth monkey doll with a feathered headdress.

"My bonus gift," she said, chuckling. "I can't imagine what got into me, paying that much for the ebony piece. Oh, well, at least I can give the doll to Lizzie."

After dinner that night, Laura showed her latest African *objet d'art* to her husband, Jack, four-year-old Lizzie, and eight-year-old Thomas Lester. "I knew it would be perfect right here," she said, placing the statue on the top shelf of her collector's cabinet.

"I don't like it," Lizzie said, moving away from the squatting ebony woman. "It's mean."

"It's just a piece of wood, honey," her mother explained. "A piece of wood can't *be* anything."

That is what the spirit wants you to think.

Lizzie held to her conviction. "I still don't like it."

"Well, maybe you'll like this," Laura said, giving Lizzie the little feathered monkey doll.

Lizzie hugged it to her chest. "Oh! I do! I'll call him Mr. Feathers. Thank you, thank you, thank you," she sang.

It was good to see her child happy. The move had been hard on both children, because it had meant leaving their grandparents and friends. That's why Laura had decided not to teach during the summer. After school was over next week, she planned to fritter away the whole summer with her family—while fixing up the Jewel Box, the nickname she'd given their turn-of-the-century house.

The wonderful old Victorian they'd just moved into was suffering from tacky decorating and neglect—a severe change from their modern split-level in Houston. But the huge rooms, high ceilings, bay windows, and four fireplaces had so many possibilities. Right away Laura had attacked the drab walls with bright paint and colorful wallpaper. Slowly the old Jewel Box was beginning to look like a real gem.

That night Laura graded papers until late. Before going to bed, she went downstairs to check the doors and shut off the lights. August came along, leading the way down the stairs. At the bottom the big cat stopped abruptly, hunched his back, and hissed.

"What is it, Brer Cat? A mouse?"

August yowled, then zipped up the stairs with his ears laid back against his head. "August," Laura said, laughing, "I didn't know you were part chicken. It's only a shadow."

A WEEK OR SO later, Laura stood at the kitchen sink watching Lizzie play in the backyard. Lizzie was singing a song she'd made up as she played. *"Mr. Feathers is my friend. August is too. They don't like the bad lady. And I don't either."*

Laura leaned over the sink to hear Lizzie better. Suddenly she felt a presence. She turned around, but there was no one there.

When she turned back to the window, a large dog had lumbered around the side of the house. It was growling and snarling angrily. Foam drooled from its mouth. Madness and pain seemed to keep it moving but with no purpose or direction. In one panic-filled moment Laura saw that the back gate had been left open.

Lizzie was still singing. Oh, no, thought Laura. Her high-pitched voice will draw the dog.

Now the dog shook its head fitfully, moving closer and closer to the sound of the singing child.

First Laura dialed 911 for help, then reached for Thomas Lester's baseball bat and quietly tiptoed to the back porch. She couldn't chance calling Lizzie, because that might make the child run. Moving instinctively, she charged out the back door, stomping and screaming to pull the dog's attention to her. It worked. The dog retreated a few steps in confusion, giving Laura a split second to put herself between her child and the attacker.

"Lizzie! Run to the porch!" she yelled. "Now!"

The child heard the urgency and fear in her mother's voice and obeyed. August bounded forward, too, and stopped in front of Laura in his stalking position. His tail twitched from side to side. The mad dog snapped and snarled, opened its jaws, and jumped forward. With legs spread apart, Laura braced for the impact.

But some unseen force seemed to snatch the dog back, holding him in place. He looked as if he were wrestling and twisting against an invisible leash.

Laura didn't take time to analyze what was happening. "Open the screen door, Lizzie," she yelled. Then scooping up August, she ran into the house. Just as Laura slammed the door the dog freed itself and in a fit of frenzy rushed at the screen. As Laura held her daughter she heard sirens announce the arrival of help.

It wasn't until the dog had been carried away that Laura let Lizzie go.

LATER THAT EVENING Laura was still shaking when she told Jack and Thomas Lester what had happened. "It couldn't attack me. It was like the dog was being held back by a powerful force."

This is a wicked thing . . .

"Where do you think the dog came from?" Thomas Lester asked, wanting to know every dramatic detail.

Very old and very powerful . . .

"It was probably a family pet, maybe trained to love and take care of a child," Jack reasoned. "So even in its diseased condition, it instinctively knew that it shouldn't attack a child. That reluctance allowed Lizzie to get to safety."

The Dabobo disguise themselves . . .

"You know how I always try to find a reasonable explanation for things," Laura said. "But for the life of me I don't know how that gate came open. I know it was locked."

Jack gave Laura a you-only-*thought*-you-locked-it look.

"Mr. Feathers and August saved us," Lizzie announced with certainty, stroking the big cat, who was asleep in her lap.

"Listen to you!" Thomas Lester teased. "That dog would've swallowed August whole."

"No way," Lizzie insisted.

"Lizzie's right," Laura said, winking. "You would've been so proud of August. He fearlessly put himself between the dog and me. Oh, and I'm sure Mr. Feathers helped out, too."

"Yo, August! Think you bad now, huh?" Thomas Lester said, giving the cat a rub behind his ears.

Everyone laughed, but in bed that night Laura lay awake replaying the strange scene in her mind—the open gate, the mad dog, dear brave August. I never knew a cat could be that protective, she thought.

OVER THE NEXT few weeks all kinds of unsettling events took place. Laura watched as family pictures mysteriously fell off the stairway wall one after the other. Then things started disappearing and showing up in the oddest places, like her keys, which she found in the freezer.

Once you willingly take it into your home, you unlock its rage . . .

Jack complained that things were breaking faster than he could fix them. And Laura felt watched all the time—just like the morning the mad dog had shown up in the yard. Sometimes she even saw movement out of the corner of her eye, but when she looked, there was nothing. And the house itself changed. Light seemed to avoid the rooms, regardless of how sunny it was outside.

Lizzie stopped going into the living room, and when Laura asked her why, she answered, "Mr. Feathers told me not to."

"Why would Mr. Feathers care, honey?"

"That's why." And Lizzie pointed to the curio cabinet with the statue of the squatting ebony woman inside. "He doesn't like her."

"And you don't either, do you?"

"No, Mama. That's not how she really looks, you know. A mean, ugly witch lives inside." And clutching the little feathered monkey doll, the child hurried away.

Lizzie was getting some strange ideas, thought Laura, deciding to monitor her daughter's television programs more closely.

You and your family could be in grave danger . . .

NO SUCH LOGIC could explain away what happened to Jack one Saturday morning.

It started with Laura finding a dead bird in her bathwater. Against Lizzie's loud protests, Laura accused the cat of the mischief and banished him to the basement. Wanting to keep him company, Lizzie joined August in exile. Jack was also downstairs fixing the washer.

Suddenly Jack screamed. "Follow me," Laura ordered Thomas Lester, who had beaten her to the basement door. Moving slowly down the steep dark steps, Laura found Jack on the floor, visibly frightened.

"Lizzie and August were playing over there," he explained. His voice was shaky. "I—I was working on the machine here. I unplugged it so I could begin fixing it." He jumped to his feet and studied the renegade appliance from a careful distance. "Then for some reason the power came back on, and I was holding hot wires. But they were snatched out of my hands! I'm not kidding. They were snatched right out of my hands. Otherwise I would have been shocked to death."

"Maybe Lizzie put the plug back in, not realizing what she was doing?"

"No, she wasn't near the plug."

Laura felt her knees weaken. "Jack? Do you hear what you're saying? An unplugged washing machine cut itself on!"

She looked at the socket. The machine was unplugged. Jack hadn't imagined that part. But had he just barely escaped being electrocuted?

You and your family could be in grave danger . . .

"Weird stuff," Thomas Lester put in. "Is this place haunted?"

Laura flinched at the sound of the word. *Haunted.* Were such things possible?

"No, son," Laura answered. "Living in old houses like this sometimes makes you *think* they're haunted, but ghosts don't exist."

"Mr. Feathers saved you, Daddy," Lizzie said, cradling the little monkey doll in her arms. And she and August ran up the steps.

Keep it with you . . .

Early the next week Thomas Lester called from the YMCA, where he spent the summer mornings. He was going on a field trip to Shaw Gardens and needed his antitoxin medicine in case a bee stung him. On the way home from the Y, Laura passed the Mother Africa Shop. She decided to go in.

"I'm Laura Bates and I bought a little figurine from you about six weeks ago. If you remember, I'd like to speak to you about it."

The woman nodded. "I remember you. I remember you didn't heed my warning. You're having trouble in your house, right?"

"I think the power of suggestion has caused me to blow ordinary occurrences out of proportion."

"Believe what you will." Mrs. Aswadi offered Laura a seat. "But hear this.

"Long ago some of the women from the village of Dabobo tricked the mother spirit into giving them immortality. Upon discovering she had been tricked, the angry goddess punished the entire village by causing terrible plagues. The innocent suffering villagers searched for the source of the goddess's anger. When they learned what some of the women had done, they drove them into the dark jungle. No one would help these women, for fear the mother spirit would turn her wrath on them. The women wandered endlessly without rest, getting older and older and older, yet unable to die. You see, they had forgotten to ask the mother spirit for eternal youth. These women were called the Dabobo women of darkness."

Mrs. Aswadi took a book from a nearby shelf. Finding the page she wanted, she pointed to a picture and said, "See. Here is an artist's carving of a Dabobo in her last human form."

Laura studied the image of the wizened old woman whose features hardly resembled those of a human. She swallowed hard. "Th-this doesn't look like the little statue I bought," she said.

"After centuries, the Dabobo women wasted away—and only their anger and meanness survived. They disguised themselves in many different forms to gain entry into a home."

"Why?"

"To take from you what was taken from them."

The room felt hot and stuffy to Laura. She wiped her brow. "Tell me about the little monkey figure with the feathered headdress."

Mrs. Aswadi reached inside her pocket and pulled out a doll just like Mr. Feathers. "This is a gingi, also very old and very powerful. In this form it is merely a trinket. But pure love unlocks its powers. Like the Dabobo, it too can take on many different forms when it is protecting or defending its owner against harm. I pray you still have the gingi I gave you, because as sure as I live, you took a Dabobo home with you."

"I gave the gingi to my little girl."

"Good. Children can unlock the protective powers of the gingi long before an adult."

"Why didn't you tell me all this before?"

"Would you have believed me? Do you believe me now?"

Mrs. Aswadi was right, and Laura left the shop not knowing what to think. Had she stumbled on to something old and dangerously wicked? And had her arrogance stopped her from admitting it? She remembered Lizzie's words: *A mean, ugly witch lives inside.*

"No," Laura said, stopping the car but completely unaware of how she'd driven home. "I will not believe it!"

You and your family could be in grave danger . . .

"I will not fall for that nonsense," she said. Later that evening Laura slipped into Lizzie's room and took Mr. Feathers from under the sleeping child's pillow. August, who slept at Lizzie's feet, woke up, stretched, then followed Laura out of the room. "We'll replace this creepy thing with something much healthier tomorrow."

With a single purpose, Laura hurried down the stairs, stopped by the curio cabinet, and took out the ebony figurine. August waited at the back door. Once outside, she poured lighter fluid on both figures and burned them in the barbecue. "So much for superstitions and hauntings," she said as she marched back to the house.

August lingered to chase a moving shadow. Suddenly he stiffened and hissed. "Come on, boy," Laura called.

"HYSTERIA! THAT's what it was." Laura paced back and forth as she told Jack about her talk with Mrs. Aswadi. "I just got caught up in her story, and when she showed me the picture of a Dabobo, I let the power of suggestion twist my thoughts into believing there might be one trying to hurt us and a gingi trying to protect us."

Laura flopped onto the bed. "Add superstition to a few odd coincidences, combine that with a child's imagination and an old house. What do you get? A haunting! Well, I just got all that junk out of my house!"

Jack looked concerned. "You've managed to explain away your fear very well. But I don't know what to do about my own. I can't dismiss what happened in the basement. It may not have anything to do with things that go bump in the night, but something far out of the ordinary happened down there."

"A freak accident. Electricity is weird anyway."

"But there's more. I didn't say anything because I didn't want to scare you."

"Stop, Jack. We are intelligent, logical-thinking people. Please don't change on me now."

"No. You need to know this," he said. "One night Lizzie told me that a bad lady was in the figurine downstairs and wanted to hurt us."

"She probably saw something on television that upset her."

"I'm not so sure. When I asked Lizzie to tell me what she'd seen, she described a toothless hag with milky eyes. She'd never heard about the Dabobo women of darkness and neither had I until tonight."

"Please, Jack. No more."

"Why are you afraid, Laura? You know what I'm going to say. I've seen the same terrible specter. And my guess is that you've—"

Before he could finish, the bedroom door burst open.

Seeing Lizzie rush in, they laughed at their own jitters. Then they noticed her expression. "Mr. Feathers says something bad has happened to Thomas Lester," she cried, holding tight to August.

Laura started to explain that Mr. Feathers was gone, but Jack had already bounded off the bed and was heading for his son's room.

"Thomas Lester," he called at the closed door. "Son? Are you awake?"

Laura and Lizzie stood by watching. Jack called again. No answer. The door was locked. But none of their doors had locks. Jack put his full weight against the door and crashed into the room. The boy lay on the floor beside his bed. His chest heaved as he struggled to breathe. Perspiration covered his forehead.

Without saying a word, the parents knew what was wrong. Thomas Lester was having an allergic reaction to a bee sting, and by the swellings on his leg, he'd been stung by more than one. Laura looked around, but she didn't see bees anywhere.

She rushed to her bathroom to get the antitoxin medicine. It wasn't there . . . or in any of the drawers . . . or on the dresser . . .

or on the nightstands. . . . Her heart was beating in her ears.

Think! she told herself. I took a bottle to the Y. But I always keep two in the house. One upstairs and one downstairs. Maybe I put them both in the kitchen cabinet. I'll look down there.

Laura clicked the switch, but the hall and stair bulbs popped out. Using the light that filtered from the bedrooms, she inched down the steps.

Grave danger . . .

"Please hurry!" Jack called.

One bee sting wasn't enough to kill the boy, but multiple stings might send him into convulsions.

Suddenly something dreadfully cold pushed past Laura. Throwing her body against the railing to regain her balance, she felt another push—harder this time! Laura turned to face her attacker.

There was the toothless hag. Its glowing silver eyes chilled Laura's soul. "Did you really think you could get rid of me by burning that little statue?" the thing snarled. "I can't be reasoned away."

Laura closed her eyes and recoiled in fear. "No. This can't be," she whispered.

"Run, Mama!" Lizzie shouted from the top of the stairs. "That's the bad woman."

Laura turned to go back for her daughter, but she lost her footing and tumbled head over heels down the steps. The hag laughed wildly and vanished.

Searing pain ripped through Laura's back like a hot iron. She dragged herself up and leaned against a nearby wall. "Thomas Lester," she whispered. "Got to help."

The Dabobo leaped at her from the darkness, screaming madly, "I'll destroy you!" The evil within it glowed.

"Leave my mama alone!" Lizzie shouted. The child had made

her way down the dark steps. Big, gray August sat beside his young mistress, his tail twitching and his ears laid back. He looked ready for battle. "Mr. Feathers won't let you hurt us anymore," Lizzie said confidently.

"Lizzie, go back. I burned the gingi—Mr. Feathers." Laura wanted to scream for Jack, but the pain in her back checked her cries.

"No, Mama. Mr. Feathers is inside August."

Suddenly August sprang at the menacing creature. As he did, his little cat body changed into a life-size gingi.

"You meddler! I'll be rid of you soon enough." The Dabobo woman scowled and melted into the darkness. The gingi followed in its new form. And every light in the house went out.

Using moonlight as his only source of illumination, Jack came down the steps, carrying Thomas Lester in his arms.

"My God, what happened?" he said, finding Laura and Lizzie huddled at the bottom of the stairs.

"Is Thomas Lester okay?" Laura gasped.

"I found the medicine in the cabinet where we always keep it," Jack answered, looking around. "What went on?"

"Get us out of here—*now!*"

Jack moved without question, swiftly carrying Lizzie and Thomas Lester to the car. Then he returned for Laura. "We're never coming back into this house again," he said. "Where's August?"

Laura didn't answer. On the way out the door she looked over Jack's shoulder. In the pale moonlight she saw two shadows locked in combat—the Dabobo trying to free itself from the grip of the gingi.

The Chicken-Coop Monster

The final story in this collection is different from the rest, because it is semi-autobiographical. I was shattered when my parents divorced, but fortunately I had a loving grandmother and grandfather who helped me through that very difficult time; I've tried to recapture a sense of that relationship here. A West African proverb from the Benin culture—"Fear is the parent of monsters"—has been used as the story's foundation, but there is a Jewish saying that is its capstone: "Love drives out fear."

THE YEAR I turned nine, my parents' ten-year marriage ended in divorce. The grownups never talked about it around me, but I knew what was going on. Mama and Daddy didn't love each other anymore. So where'd that leave me?

As soon as school was out, they shipped me off to the Tennessee boonies to stay with my grandparents, Franky and James Leon Russell. I didn't want to go, but no one was listening to me.

A monster lived there. I knew it the minute I set foot on their farm. I was the president of the St. Louis chapter of the Monster Watchers of America, and I was an expert on spotting monsters.

It lived in the chicken coop—the tingling in the back of my neck was strongest when I passed by there. Its hot, mean eyes watched me as I played on the back porch. Sometimes I chased my ball too close and smelled its foul breath. This wasn't an ordinary in-the-closet fright or an under-the-bed scare. I'd come upon something really terrible.

I needed help with this one, so I wrote to my friend Jay, who was in charge of the MWA over the summer. Jay and I had been best buddies since we'd started the MWA the year before. By enclosing fifty cents and six box tops from Crinkle cereal, we'd sent away for and received an official MWA Club starter kit, complete with six badges, six glow-in-the-dark ID cards, and a manual containing ten monster rules and everything else we needed to know about creepy stuff. We'd invited Nora, Jeff, Latisha, and Alandro to join us.

Writing to Jay made me feel better. Meanwhile, I had to be careful not to break any monster rules, because that would make the thing stronger and bolder.

One evening Ma Franky called me to the kitchen. "Missy, I forgot to throw the latch on the chicken coop. Go lock it for me, please."

The sun had set, but there was a little light left in the sky. The backyard was already engulfed by a blanket of darkness, but I could see the silhouette of the old chicken shack against the sky.

I stood on the back porch, a statue of fear. This is what the monster had been waiting for. I heard the whisper of its tail swishing in the straw.

"Melissa?" My own name startled me. "Why haven't you done what I asked you to do?" Ma Franky's voice quavered with impatience.

She was asking me to break monster rule number five: *Get in the house before dark and don't go out by yourself.*

"There's a monster in your chicken coop," I blurted out. "So I'm not going out there."

Of course Ma Franky had other ideas. "Girl," she said, "if you don't stop this foolishness!" She gave me a little push. "Go on, now. Go close the door, or something will get in the coop and scare my setting hens."

Her hens? What about me? "I hate to tell you this, Ma Franky, but something's in the chicken coop already. That's why I'm not going out there."

"Yes you are, this very minute."

Obviously this monster had fourth-level power, because it'd put a spell on Ma Franky. Why else would she fall for the oldest trick in the book? *Monsters make helpers out of unsuspecting victims.*

"But—" I started to say.

"No buts!" And the next thing I knew, my own grandmother had me by the hand and was pulling me toward the chicken coop. "I want to show you there's nothing out here."

I looked into her eyes. "No!" I screamed. "Don't you see? It's made you a helper." I jerked away from Ma Franky and ran into the house. Even though I was breaking monster rule three—*Never let a monster see you crying*—I couldn't stop the tears.

Then I felt big, strong hands wiping my face with a cool washcloth. "Oh, sweets," Daddy James whispered softly. "There's nothing round here to fear." His eyes smiled. The monster spell hadn't gotten to him. "No need to fret. I closed the door for you."

DARK THOUGHTS flee in morning light. But the old wooden coop was surrounded by permanent shadows, a sure sign that it was occupied by a hateful thing. I had to be very careful. It would do anything to lure me into its evil hole.

"Bring me my clothespins off the porch," Ma Franky called.

Just as I passed the coop the door creaked open slowly. Sunlight pushed away the darkness just long enough for me to see something large and shapeless. But the monster leaped back into the shadows before I got a really good look at it. I must have screamed, 'cause Ma Franky came running.

"What is it? What is it?"

"I saw the monster. It pushed open the door."

Ma Franky said nothing but walked purposefully into the coop. I wouldn't look, *couldn't* look as she disappeared behind the darkness. I never expected to see her again. But within a few seconds out she came holding a tiny little chick.

She gently transferred it from her hands to mine. "But that isn't the monster," I cried.

"I know. There isn't one. Period!"

Poor Ma Franky. She really believed that, I'm sure. "Won't you come in and look around?" she asked. "Come see where the chickens set on their eggs and hatch little chicks like this one."

It was another monster trick, and I wasn't going for it. "No! I'll never go inside!"

Ma Franky sighed and shook her head. "Whenever you're ready,"

she said, and went back to hanging out her wash. My back was turned, but I could feel the creature laughing at me.

DURING THE WEEK, separate letters came from Mama and Daddy. I wrote them back right away—Mama's went to our old house, Daddy's to a new address. Mama wanted to know all about my new friends. Daddy was happy I could swim in deep water and had caught a fish. But I still hadn't heard from Jay, so I wrote to him again.

First I told him about my new pet chick, Tissy, and how she followed me everywhere, answering my voice and eating the feed I threw out to her. Then I told him about the creature. "I feel it's stronger now, because I've broken a couple of monster rules. It's a tricky one, but I'm watching out for myself. Write soon. Missy."

Following rule nine, I didn't go near the thing's lair. In fact I didn't even play in the backyard. But late one afternoon I missed Tissy. I felt she was in danger. Sure enough, the chick was out back, heading straight for the coop. And the door was open!

Tissy belonged to me. The monster knew it. Monster rule six clearly stated: *Watch out for those you love. If monsters can't get you, they will get the ones closest to you.*

If little Tissy went inside, she was a goner! I had to do something—and fast.

"Here, biddy-biddy-biddy." I imitated Ma Franky calling her hens. Tissy heard my voice and stopped. That was the split second I needed. Dashing forward, I scooped up my little chick and swerved to keep from plunging headlong into the monster's den.

No tears this time. I was mad, so I foolishly broke rule ten—*never let the monster see you angry.*

"Hey, Chicken Neck! You're a real creep, Creep! Why pick on a little bitty innocent chick? Mess with somebody your own size!"

Like who did I have in mind? How dumb could I get? My anger had made the monster swell with fresh power. If I kept breaking rules like that, the creepy thing was going to get me for sure.

AT LAST a letter came from Jay.

July 18, 1960

Dear Missy,

Never got your first letter. The monster must have eaten it. Beware!

The MWA met today. I read your letter to them. We all agreed you're okay as long as you don't break rule one: *Don't face a monster alone!*

The MWA went to see *The Werewolf Returns* five times. We're going again today. We miss you. Come home soon.

Your friend,
Jay

P.S. Are you going to bring Tissy with you?

Hearing from Jay and my friends helped ease my mind a little. The MWA was right. Nothing could happen to me unless I made the number-one mistake. So I stayed on my guard, ready for any tricks.

That evening the six Harper kids came down to play hide-and-seek. Mae Lizabeth, who was my age but three times my size, smelled like lilac talcum powder all the time. She had a likable way about her that made me feel comfortable. During the summer we had become almost friends.

"Come be my partner and hide with me," I said.

Mae Lizabeth pulled me along behind her. I suggested we hide behind the shrubs along the front porch.

"Come on," she said. "Let's hide in the chicken coop!"

I jerked away. "No! Don't . . ."

"Why? It's the perfect place to hide." Suddenly my almost-friend rushed toward that dreaded spot.

I could feel the monster's excitement. My warnings didn't stop Mae Lizabeth from going inside. When she disappeared into the darkness, I started screaming. At the same time Mae Lizabeth let go a bloodcurdling cry. I knew without a doubt my friend had been devoured.

Daddy James, moving like a man half his age, reached the backyard first. Ma Franky puffed along behind him fussing, "We're too old to be going through this, James."

Mae Lizabeth staggered forward, terror and pain twisting her face. She was holding her arm. Blood oozed from a deep gash and trickled down her hand.

Well, the monster hadn't swallowed Mae Lizabeth, but he'd taken a good-size bite out of her arm. Actually, I felt relieved. Now everybody would know that I'd been right all along.

Ma Franky scooted me off to the house to get the first-aid kit. "Seems this nail scratched you," she was saying when I got back. And Daddy James looked and nodded his agreement.

A nail? Oh, no! They couldn't be faked out by that old monster trick. No nail had attacked Mae Lizabeth. I moved in close to get a good look at the wound. "It was the monster!" I shouted. "I bet he did this with his sharp claws. Tell them, Mae Lizabeth. Tell them!"

Mae Lizabeth's eyes opened wide. "Huh? Oh, yes, I saw it . . . It got me."

The monster was hiding deep in the shadows, but I felt it stir. Oh, no, I thought. I was breaking monster rule seven: *Never lie about seeing a monster.* I hadn't lied, but I'd made my friend lie.

"Stop, Mae Lizabeth. You didn't really see anything, did you?" said Daddy James.

The girl shook her head.

"And neither did you, Missy," Ma Franky put in. "Tell me the truth. Have you ever really *seen* anything in that coop?"

"No," I answered, but hurried on to add, "That's how they fool you."

"Hush! Hush this minute," Ma Franky said sternly. "There's nothing in that old coop to hurt anybody."

"Oh, yeah?" I sassed back. "Well, what's that running down Mae Lizabeth's arm? Tomato juice?"

Daddy James pulled me behind him. "Don't speak to your grandmama that way," he said in a stern voice.

"I'm sorry for sassing Ma Franky." And I really was sorry. Lies. Sassing. None of this was me! That thing in the coop had made my summer miserable. I wanted to hate it, but that would break rule eight.

The Harper children stared in wide-eyed amazement while Ma Franky bandaged Mae Lizabeth's arm. Then Daddy James and I walked them home.

"It's a water moon," he said on the way back, pointing out how hazy the full moon looked. "It'll rain 'fore morning."

Most of the time Daddy James was right about things like that. He had his own way of understanding the world, and he'd taught me how to see things differently, too.

For a while we walked in silence. "Missy," he said at last. "Tell me about the monster in your grandmama's chicken coop."

What? Was my very own grandfather a believer? I tested him. "Ma Franky doesn't think it exists."

"I know. But monsters are sneaky like that," he said. "They want people not to believe in them."

How lucky could a kid get? My grandfather knew about monster tricks. He listened while I talked about Jay, the MWA, and all ten monster rules.

"I've never really seen the thing in the coop, but I can feel it. And once this summer I saw its shadow. It was big! Since it lives in a chicken coop, I bet it looks a lot like a big chicken."

"Makes sense."

"I imagine it's got two big yellow eyes that glow in the dark, razor-sharp scales, and three-fingered claw hands and claw feet. It stinks like a sewer."

"That sounds like a pretty powerful monster," he said, chuckling softly. "It was a long, long time ago, but a monster like that lived in the crawlspace under my house."

"Really?"

"The thing had me so scared I couldn't even play in my own yard. Then one night I decided to face my monster."

"You broke monster rule one?"

Daddy James laughed. "Is that the rule that says you shouldn't face a monster alone?" I nodded. He went on. "'Spec I did. But to keep that ol' slinky, slimy thing from beatin' me down, I had to take it on face to face."

"Was it ugly?"

"It was all the way ugly!"

"Was it mean?"

"Oooo-weeee. It was mean like a snake. But I found courage that night long ago."

"Tell me what happened!"

"I called that monster out, and when it came, I stood flatfooted and looked at it straight in the face."

"Weren't you scared?"

"At first. But as I held my ground I got stronger and it got weaker. Then I said, 'I'm not afraid of you. Now git gone!' Next thing I knew, it had run off hollering."

"Did it ever come back?"

"Oh, every now and then one tries to scare me. But that monster long ago must have told all its friends that I wasn't easy to scare, 'cause I ain' been bothered too much down through the years . . . till now, that is."

I was so excited. Daddy James was a monster fighter. "Good! Then will you chase the creepy thing in the chicken coop away?"

"I could. But it ain' troubling me. If I run it off, it'll just come back and devil you some other way. To be rid of it forever, you must call it out and face it by yourself."

"You mean break monster rules one and two? That'd be like facing Dracula in his castle, at night, all by myself! I wouldn't have a chance."

"You can do it. You're my granddaughter, and that makes you very special."

The short walk home had taken over an hour. Ma Franky had homemade peach ice cream waiting. I didn't feel much like eating, knowing what was before me.

Mustering my courage, I hugged Ma Franky and Daddy James, just in case I didn't get back. "There is no fear in love," he whispered.

Breaking every rule in the monster manual and trusting my grandfather completely, I went to face the creature within.

"You Chicken Creep. Come out and face me."

Heat lightning zippered across the sky. Thunder grumbled in the distance. Slowly the coop door creaked open. The monster's foul odor sprang at me from its dark hole. The wind picked up, sending wind eddies scampering in the dust. All at once a scratchy moan followed by an awful commotion chilled me to the bone. "Ssss-flip-kkkkk-flop, ssss-flop-kkkkk-flop!" The thing was at the door. I waited breathlessly, not knowing what to expect. Running crossed my mind, but Daddy James's words helped me stand firm. And I did.

What a surprise to see Ma Franky's rooster flap and flutter out of the dark hole with one of his feet stuck in a tin can.

"Another trick," I said boldly. "You can't distract me."

The wind whipped and churned the trees. The thing's anger roared out of the dark gaping hole. It wanted to get me. Why wouldn't it come? Suddenly I realized it couldn't! I was getting stronger and it was getting weaker.

Armed with the powerful weapon my grandfather had given me, I yelled over the whistling wind, "I'm not afraid of you. You're just a lot of hot stinky air."

I heard scurrying about inside the darkness. I waited and waited, hardly noticing that it had started to rain.

Then calling upon the growing courage within me, I turned my back on the monster, saying with confidence, "I am the oldest granddaughter of James Leon Russell. He loves me, and I know it!"

And that's when I knew that my monster was gone!